SECRETS, LIES, AND TEMPTATION

A FORBIDDEN AGE GAP ROMANCE

L.A. ROCK SCENE

MELANIE A. SMITH

WICKED DREAMS PUBLISHING

Published by
WICKED DREAMS PUBLISHING
info@wickeddreamspublishing.com
Boise, ID USA

Cover design, editing, and formatting by Wicked Dreams Publishing

eBook ISBN: 978-1-952121-71-5
Paperback ISBN: 978-1-952121-89-0
Discreet Paperback ISBN: 978-1-952121-95-1
Hardback ISBN: 978-1-952121-96-8

CONTENTS

CONTENT WARNING

Secrets, Lies, and Temptation is a forbidden age gap romance novel that includes elements that might not be suitable for some readers, including the use of profanity, open-door sex scenes, and other potentially sensitive topics. For a full list visit: https://melanieasmithauthor.com/sltcw.html

PLAYLIST

To listen along, check out the *Secrets, Lies, and Temptation Playlist on Spotify*

The Steam

Do I Wanna Know by Arctic Monkeys

Need You Tonight by INXS

Closer by Nine Inch Nails

Wicked Game by Chris Isaak

The Romance

Glycerine by Bush

Help Me Be Good to You by Heather Nova

I'd Do Anything for Love (But I Won't Do That) by Meatloaf

It's Only Love by Heather Nova

Everlong by Foo Fighters

The Journey

Girls Just Wanna Have Fun by Cyndi Lauper

Criminal by Fiona Apple

Little Earthquakes by Tori Amos

Losing My Religion by R.E.M.

Shake it Out by Florence + The Machine

1

NILS

"You sure you've got this handled?" Frankie asks me for the tenth time this afternoon.

I smirk at her from the leather chair across her giant desk. "Of course I do. Now go home already."

She lifts a dark eyebrow and purses her bright red lips. "I think you've taken a little too well to running the joint."

I shrug, fighting a smile. "Maybe."

She nods slowly. "You're good at it, you know."

My eyebrows jump. It's rare that a compliment falls from those luscious lips of hers. "Thank you," I reply with quiet surprise.

"In fact, I was hoping …" She trails off, then shakes her head. "Nah, never mind. You're probably not up for the challenge."

That gets a chuckle out of me. "I'm not your two-year-old, Francesca. Reverse psychology won't work on me."

"Clearly, since you used my full name, you cheeky bastard," she teases with a wink.

"What is it you need?" I ask pointedly.

Frankie taps a red fingernail on the desk. "You know we're closing on Allure next month."

I nod. There's no way I could forget Frankie and Julian's third acquisition, a nightclub about a half mile from Frankie's first club, Baltia — this club — and a bit more than that from her second, Los Jardines. I've been wondering when she'd ask me to handle the takeover, just as I did with Los Jardines.

"And?" I prompt, bemused. I don't usually have to pull things out of her like this. Frankie never has a problem saying exactly what she wants. One of the many things I admire about her.

"And … I'd like you to train Emma before the transition."

I can't help the confused look I give her. "Emma? As in, your best friend, Emma?" She nods in confirmation. "To do what?" I ask baldly. Emma is all curves and sass, and usually only around for the free drinks Frankie allows her. I never knew her to have any ambition beyond being a hairdresser.

"To manage it," she replies. I open my mouth to protest but Frankie throws up a hand. "I know she won't be ready to take full responsibility for running a club after a month. But that's the end goal, down the road."

"*Far* down the road," I grumble under my breath.

Frankie smiles tolerantly. "She's smarter than you think, and she's used to working her ass off. Give her a shot. Please. If you don't see potential in her to at least be an assistant manager in three months … well, we'll go from there. But I promise I won't stick you with her forever if it's not working for you."

I study Frankie shrewdly for a moment. "Did she ask for this?" I finally respond.

Frankie examines her fingernails, avoiding eye contact. "No. I asked her." Her dark eyes flick back up to meet mine and I see anxiety there. "I need more people in this that I trust if we're going to keep expanding. It hit us hard when Annika left, and Johnny's got his hands full with Los Jardines, even with your help. I don't want to bring in someone new right now. Someone I won't be sure will stick around."

I process that for a moment. "Fair enough." I don't voice that with two kids, one right after the other, I know how hard this must all be for her to balance. She's barely taken any steps back, save the occasional night off like tonight so she can be with her husband and children. "I'll do my best to bring Emma into the fold."

Frankie breathes an audible sigh of relief that makes me scrutinize her closer.

"Don't look at me like that," she says, turning red.

"Like what?" I ask, genuinely unsure of what she means. I've long stopped giving her puppy-dog eyes. Equal parts because she's well and truly taken and because of whom she's taken *by*. I'd rather not get snapped in half by Julian anytime soon.

"Like I'm hiding something," she accuses me.

I raise an eyebrow at the guilt in her tone. "*Are* you hiding something?"

Frankie buries her face in her hands. "I'm pregnant again," she admits.

The shock only lasts a moment before I snort a laugh. "Of course you are. I mean, Lucia turns one tomorrow, yes? Considering she was conceived mere months after Nico came along, I'm honestly surprised it took so long."

Frankie drops her hands and gives me a mock-sour look. "So I'm fertile, sue me."

I try to hold back my amusement, but it's practically impossible. "And you two fuck like bunnies," I point out with a smirk.

Frankie rolls her eyes to the ceiling resignedly. "Yes, that we do … but I think Julian plans this shit, honestly." Her gaze drops back down. "He loves being a dad and he's so damn happy. Which is great. I just don't know how we're going to keep all this —" She gives a sweeping gesture around the room that I take to mean the club and all of her other businesses "— going with three kids. Three fucking kids, Nils." She sighs and shakes her head.

I cross one leg over the other and give her a look. "You're not happy?"

A small smile tugs at her lips. "No, I'm happy. And Nonna is over the moon. I just … I'm overwhelmed, that's all."

"And worried."

She nods. "Is it that obvious?"

I huff a breath out of my nose. "You've only asked about Violent Mood Swings' private concert tonight … oh, I don't know … fifteen times today?" I tease.

She shrugs. "It's an important event."

I narrow my eyes at her. They're all important events, to the artists anyway. And the fans. And of course, our bottom line. But as I study her, I glean that's not what she means.

"You're sad because you're going to miss it," I deduce.

Her red lips pull into a grimace. "I am. But I'm old enough to know I can't stay up until three o'clock in the morning anymore and then wake up at six a.m. with my toddlers before a birthday party full of a million other toddlers hopped up on excitement and cake." She takes a deep breath and lets it out with a heavy sigh.

"Hey," I say firmly, concerned at how over-wrought she is right now. Frankie looks up at me. "I have it on good authority that West is well and truly back on the wagon this time, and I have a feeling this is the first of many concerts for them. You'll get to see one of their performances. We'll make it happen. And in the meantime, I'll make sure all three clubs are doing well. So don't you worry about a damn thing, do you hear me?"

Frankie's eyes fill with tears, and she jumps out of her chair, rounding the desk to lean over and throw her arms around me. "Thank you," she whispers in my ear, hugging me tightly. Since she can't see me, I smile fondly. It's crazy how close we've gotten these last couple of years, especially considering our first year working together was such a rollercoaster.

"You're welcome. Now go *home*, woman. I have to help Ace get things ready."

Frankie straightens up, smiling as she wipes away the tears. "Yeah. You're right. I should go." She sniffs and wipes away her tears. "Stupid fucking pregnancy hormones."

2

ALEXSIS

"I can't do this."

I fight back a sigh and turn around to find Max stopped on the sidewalk. "You can totally do this," I reassure her. "You're a fucking badass rock journalist, girl."

She looks at me with pleading eyes. "You weren't there. West has got to be pissed at me, Alexsis. I can't distract him tonight. You go on, I'll just —"

I lean forward and put a hand over her mouth, cupping it carefully so I don't smudge her lipstick. "I did not just spend two hours doing your hair and makeup — making you look like a goddess — for you to back out now. So his apology tour has been heavy? We all knew it would be. But tonight is big for the band, so you're going in, you're going to act like everything is perfectly normal, and it'll all be just fine," I insist. "Besides, Jason will have your ass if you don't go."

Max pulls a face. "Yeah, okay, you're right."

I smirk at her. We both know our boss acts the softie when it suits him, but underneath he's all about the story. Like Max usually is, too, when she's not forced to follow her childhood rockstar crush around on his bid to redeem himself after ripping his band apart years ago. I keep that thought to myself, though.

"Damn straight. Now come on. I'll prove to you that this is going to be no big deal. In fact, you might even have some fun," I persist airily.

She leans into me and groans, but allows me to pull her along and through the doors. I push her ahead of me when I hear West's voice, then another man's after him.

"Hey, Maxi," West greets her, running a hand through his dark hair while doing surprised elevator eyes over her. I smile smugly. He gestures to the guy standing beside him. "This is Nils, Baltia's manager."

My gaze bounces from West's face at the name and lands on the other man. *Nils*? No. It can't possibly be …

But it's that tall, lean body I remember. And I'd

never forget that messy, sexy dark blond hair and those piercing blue eyes. My hands clap over my mouth.

"Oh my god, Nils Larssen?!" I flap my hands wildly, trying and failing to contain myself as West and Max both look at me like I'm nuts before exchanging a concerned look.

For his part, Nils looks at me like he's never seen me before. But then, I'm not surprised, considering.

"You don't remember me, do you?" I ask.

He studies my face for a moment before his ice-blue eyes meet mine. "I'm sorry, I don't," he replies. "You are …?"

"Alexsis Monaghan," I respond, then turn to Max since she's giving me the silent what-the-fuck-is-going-on-here vibe. "Nils was an exchange student who stayed with us … oh my gosh, what was it? Fifteen years ago?" My heart flutters at the memories of following him around for what was probably the best year of my young life.

"Holy shit." The words burst from his lips as his own memory clearly clicks into place. "Seventeen years ago," he corrects me in a hushed tone. "You were a baby. What, five years old? I'm surprised you even remember me. Now look at you."

And look at me he does. So intensely that my

skin warms under his gaze. I may have been just a child, but he was the man who fueled my childish fantasies of falling in love for *years*.

"Are you kidding? You were my first crush," I reply honestly, batting my eyelashes at him coyly. Finally. *Finally*, after all these years, I can flirt with him in real life.

"Is that so?" he murmurs in a tone that sends a fresh wave of heat over my skin.

I nod, mesmerized, vaguely registering Max and West wordlessly wandering off together, but I'm too focused on Nils to acknowledge it. "I'm surprised you didn't know. My brothers teased me horribly about it for years," I admit.

"How are Asher and Aiden?" he asks, clearly as purposefully oblivious to our friends' departures.

"They're good," I respond. "Asher is a marketing director for Lexus and Aiden is an archivist at The Getty."

Nils takes a step forward. "Impressive. And you? What is it you do, Alexsis?" he purrs, sending shivers down my back.

God, he's flirting *back*. I half want to pinch myself to make sure I'm not dreaming.

"I'm a journalist at *Rock Scene* with Max," I

respond. "I just finished college at the end of last year, though, so I'm still learning the ropes."

"Well, if you're looking for material, you're certainly in the right place. Baltia's seen it all."

What a perfect opening. I tip my head. "I bet you have, too, then."

He smiles vaguely. "I've only been in the industry just over five years. But yes, I suppose I have a few stories."

"Well, then I think I need a tour," I reply, gesturing around the club. I've been here dozens of times and I'm pretty familiar with its history, but like hell I'm going to pass up more time with him. Also, I can't help wondering how I never noticed him here all these years. Then again, I guess on some level I'd assumed the shy, Swedish boy who stole my heart had taken it back to his homeland with him.

He gives me a cryptic look but extends his arm. "Then come with me," he offers.

With a grin, I snake my arm through his and tuck in close against him. He smells like alcohol and leather. Two of my favorite things.

"Thank you," I reply. "You know, you don't even have an accent anymore."

Nils grimaces. Maybe a sore subject then. "Well,

I have been in the States as long as I lived in Sweden," he points out.

I tilt my head as we step down into the stage pit. "You haven't gone back?"

"A few times, but never for long. Your family did a good job of helping me love my new home." He looks down at me and winks. I don't miss the subtle reminder that he was basically part of my family for a time.

I try to forget that fact as he politely escorts me around the club like he's giving a formal tour, sharing with me as much history of the club as he knows. I play the game, asking thoughtful questions and giving him a chance to see that I'm not a little girl anymore. That I'm on his level now. And I am, much more so than I'd ever even dreamed, as we clearly share a love for rock of all forms.

After the tour, we get drinks and watch Violent Mood Swings' private concert together from the VIP balcony. They're good. Really good. Maybe even better than they were before. Still, having Nils by my side in the dark, high-energy club is distracting, and I can't help sneaking glances at his tall, intimidating self. He always had presence, and it seems its lure has only grown with time. I also have to fight the grin that comes to my face every time I catch him staring at me out of the corner of my eye.

Who would ever have thought that a few side glances could be so damn hot? All new fantasies bloom in my mind that I'd never had the maturity to even consider back then. And despite his trying to reel things back to a respectfully polite distance, clearly I affect him. The thought makes me a little dizzy with glee.

After it's over, though, we head downstairs so I can meet up with Max.

"Where did you two sneak off to?" she whispers in my ear as Nils leads us backstage.

I elbow her and grin. "Wouldn't you like to know? But hey, good show, right?"

Max nods, her grin sliding up to megawatt status. "*So* good."

"Great show, West," I hear Nils say. I look up to find him patting West on the back. "Can't wait for the tour."

"You and me both, dude," West replies, looking well-pleased with himself.

Max joins the conversation, and the heated looks she and West are giving each other is all the cue I need to leave. I catch Nils's eye, and he tips his head back toward the club proper. I nod subtly and he splits off from the pair, who are now talking only to each other, so I follow.

"It was great running into you," I say as we emerge back into the now-bright club.

"You, too," he replies.

Butterflies from both happiness and nerves tumble inside me.

"We should get lunch or something sometime," I offer.

I can see the hesitation in his eyes. Even though I have a few guesses as to what's causing it, it makes me want to ask why. To hear it from his lips.

But I hold back for once.

"Yes. We should. I'll give you a call sometime," he finally says.

I deflate a little. Because everyone knows the phrase "I'll give you a call sometime" is the polite way to say, "you'll never see me naked." But I give him my phone number anyway. After all, as Aristotle said, hope is a waking dream.

Lord knows I've dreamed of this man many times. And now, here he is. Our chance meeting can't be for nothing. In fact, I refuse to believe it is. So, I dare to hope.

3

NILS

FOUR MONTHS LATER

Just when I thought Violent Mood Swings was over after yet another embarrassingly messy public breakup, they pull an amazing new album out of their bag of tricks. I stand between the stairs to the stage and the entrance, listening to West and his band put it all on the line. They've got some big ones to try to win people back with a surprise album and concert, I'll give them that.

As I catalog the crowd, I don't miss that Max Marshall hangs in the back … but it takes me a moment to see that she's not alone. My chest tightens with anticipation as I catch a glimpse of Alexsis on Max's far side as she leans forward to talk to Max. I skirt forward, unconsciously trying to get a better look at her.

I can't help it. Even though I know I shouldn't, I feel myself pulled toward her. I stand at the railing to the side of the stairs and get my first full look at her in months as she sways to the music.

God, she's even more beautiful than I remembered. She's mesmerizing. Despite myself, I imagine where we'd be if I'd called her. Friends? Or maybe more … and since it's all in my head, maybe more that involves touching her soft, supple skin, running my fingers through her cornsilk blond hair …

I'm so taken with my fantasy that I miss what's happening at the door until I hear shouting behind me. My skin prickles as I turn back just in time to see a swell of bodies push into the bouncers who usually keep things in check. But it quickly becomes obvious that there aren't enough to stem the tide.

And I know in an instant that all hell is about to break loose.

An hour later, the club has been cleared of the massive crowd that broke through the door, and West has gone off to find Max and win her heart back after winning the fans' back.

I drop into the chair across from Frankie's desk tiredly. She taps her bright red fingernails on the desk, clearly disconcerted.

"Well, that fucking sucked. What promised to be one of the most iconic nights in the history of owning this club has turned into an epic financial failure courtesy of a bunch of dickwads and the overzealous LAPD."

I smile tiredly in her direction. "It'll still be iconic."

She raises an eyebrow. "Yeah, I guess you're right." Then she looks at me in that way she does. The look I call the Frankie Detector. Not that I'd ever speak those words aloud. "Where were you when that shit was going down at the door?"

I raise a brow back. "What makes you think I wasn't at the door?"

The slant of her eyebrow steepens with disbelief, and it makes me chuckle.

"I was watching the crowd," I offer. And it's true. Even if it was just one member of the crowd.

"I have a feeling you're leaving something out," she presses.

There's The Detector. I suppress a sigh. "I was watching a woman, if you must know. I'm sorry, I should've been there to put a stop to it."

She waves a hand dismissively and leans back in her chair with a sigh. "If five bouncers and Julian couldn't, I doubt there would've been much you could've done to stop it." She examines me for a moment. "So, a woman, huh? This wouldn't be West's girl's blonde friend, would it?"

I shake my head and laugh. Francesca Greco doesn't miss a goddamn thing. I pity her children growing up with a mother that knows their every move before they even make it.

"Yes," I reply simply.

She nods slowly. "You like her."

I cut a sharp gaze at her. "Your point?"

"I think you know my point," she replies, her lips parting in a grin. "Not still carrying a torch for me, are you?" She winks at me.

I narrow my eyes, and my mouth tightens into a thin line. She knows I'll always want her on some level. But I've resigned myself to looking but never touching. Unfortunately, once you've fallen for someone like Frankie, it's hard to find other women as exciting.

And yet, I haven't stopped thinking about Alexsis since she popped back into my life. I know I shouldn't. It's why I haven't contacted her. She's young. Far too young. And it feels like an insult to the family who gave me footing here to turn around and lust after their baby girl. Even if our reunion left me with nightly dreams about her. I know I probably just need to get laid, but nobody else has been able to take my mind off of her. Not since she popped back into my life, then left an Alexsis-shaped hole in it.

That right there should've gotten my attention. There's something special about Alexsis that makes me want to set aside our twelve-year age difference and all the other reasons for not pursuing her.

"No," I murmur eventually. "No, I'm not. And I do know your point, but I can't have her. Same as I can't have you." I let the seriousness of my words hang in the air, but I don't look at her.

"Nils."

I sigh and raise my gaze to Frankie's.

"Quit being such a martyr and go get the goddamn girl."

"It's not that simple."

"What, does she bat for the other team or something?"

"No, she doesn't," I respond with a small smile. At least I know that much from the looks and touches she'd given me. Ones that didn't make my decision any easier.

"Is she into you?"

I roll my eyes to the ceiling. "I think so, yes." At least, she was months ago.

"Then I seriously don't know why we're having this conversation. Get off your reserved Swedish ass and do something about it."

I open my mouth to protest. To explain. But then … I realize maybe she's right. So Alexsis is young. So I stayed with her family ages ago. We're both adults now. And if her reappearance reminded me of anything, it's that I haven't stopped thinking about her. Why *am* I torturing myself like this?

There's something there. And if just the sight of her does things to me … well, I owe it to both of us to see why that is, don't I? I've certainly been with people, men and women, that I was less attracted to than Alexsis. And I'm rarely drawn to anyone the way I'm drawn to her.

Frankie is right. I was martyring myself over this. But maybe I don't need to. Maybe it would be okay to at least see if there might really be something between us before I go off the deep end.

I rise, giving a small shrug. "All right, if you insist." I turn and slide a hand into my pocket, strolling out the door casually to Frankie's laughter behind me.

"Atta boy. And don't come back until you've had a piece of that ass!" she calls after me.

I let the smile pull at my lips this time. Because as much as I'd enjoy doing exactly that, I have a feeling there's so much more to this thing between Alexsis and me.

4

ALEXSIS

I'm in the middle of a meeting when my phone pings with a text message.

Still up for lunch or something?

Just when I'd finally put Nils Larsson out of my mind. I stare down at my phone and shake my head in annoyance.

"What?" Max asks from across a table full of research ahead of our interview with Dermot Kennedy.

I was so jazzed a minute ago because interviewing him is monumental, not just because I'm a huge fan and this could be amazing for my career, but also for the magazine. Unfortunately, Nils's text has fully squashed that feeling, and I can't help the frown that pulls at my lips.

"It's nothing," I murmur.

Max smirks at me. "I know that look. That's the boy trouble look. Is it that guy that stood you up this weekend?"

I roll my eyes. "I already blocked him, so no." Another internet date flop I'd mentally dismissed. I worry my bottom lip between my teeth as I debate whether to say anything about Nils. Because Max was so insistent for weeks after running into each other that he was into me. I know anything I say will just restart that whole shtick.

Max just stares at me expectantly, one brow raised. And I cave because I can't not talk about this.

"Fine, it was Nils. He wants to know if I want to have lunch or something."

"And that's a bad thing?"

"No," I admit grudgingly. "I guess it's not."

"You're annoyed it took him so long," Max says. Not asks.

"Of course I am. But you know. He's a busy guy. I'm a busy gal. Whatever." I cringe internally at how obviously non-genuine that sounded.

Max folds her long fingers together under her chin. "Then I assume you're going to say yes?"

I scrunch my nose. Even though I never said it out loud, she knows what running into him again after all these years did to me. Even I could feel the stars in my eyes that day. Ugh, it's his fault for still being so damn handsome and charming and dangerously alluring. Even if I wanted to play hard to get, which I wouldn't anyway since I'm not that type, I already know I'm going to say yes. And so does Max. She just wants to hear me say it.

"Of course," I reply with exasperation. She claps her hands gleefully. "Even though it's almost insulting how long he waited to ask, if I said anything …" I trail off, my eyes going wide.

"He'd know how into him you really are? It's okay, I already know. You can say it out loud." Max winks at me.

"Yeah okay, fine, I'm into him, all right? But it's just lunch *or something.*" I don't know why I say it sarcastically, since I'm pretty sure they were my words to begin with.

"Mm hmm," Max hums. "We'll see."

I stare at her across the table, torn between wanting to point out that someone who's into you doesn't wait this long to ask you out and … well, hoping she's right.

Before I walk into the diner across from Baltia, I rub my sweaty palms on my pants. I may be dressed casually in a pink vee-neck tee, dark skinny jeans, and black low-top Chucks with my blond hair pulled up into a ponytail, but the pounding of my heart is anything but casual. I take a deep breath to steady myself and head inside.

I spot him immediately at a booth on the left side of the dingy little restaurant. His long, lithe frame is leaned back into the blue upholstered booth, his legs stretched out under the table. His shaggy blond hair falls over his forehead in the same reckless way it always has. But the short beard is new. And fucking hot.

I take another deep breath and slap a smile on my face as I approach.

"Nils," I call. "Hey!"

He looks up, then rises from the booth to meet me. I'm surprised when he leans down and kisses my cheek. Besides the soft press of his lips sending my insides tumbling, his amazing smell sets my head spinning.

So, when he pulls back and looks down at me with a smile, I stare blankly back up at him.

"It's good to see you." He gestures to the seat

across from where he'd been sitting. "I'm glad you could join me."

I can feel the blush on my cheeks as I slide into the booth. "I'm glad you texted." He settles back into his seat. "Though I was a little surprised, honestly."

The corner of his mouth quirks up. "Oh? Why's that?"

"It had just been a while. I figured I wasn't going to hear from you." I pick up a menu from the holder against the wall, willing myself to stop saying every stupid thing that passes through my mind.

Nils taps his finger thoughtfully on the table in front of him. "Honestly," he says, clearly borrowing my use of the word, "I didn't think you were going to hear from me either." He leans forward, lacing his fingers together. "I didn't know if this sort of thing would be … appropriate."

I glance down at the menu, blushing again. Dammit. Since when do I blush?

"How so?" I ask, looking up at him from under my eyelashes.

His ice-blue eyes scan my face, making me blush even deeper. Jesus, his gaze has a way of wreaking havoc on me.

"Well, I *am* quite a bit older than you."

That gets my attention. My eyes open wide as I

look back at him. *That's* what's bothering him about this? If he thinks age matters here, then …

"Nils, is this a date?"

The tilt of his lips deepens into the hint of a smile. "That's a very forward question."

I laugh. "Well, one of us has to be," I reply. "And you've always been quiet. So, I guess it's up to me."

Now Nils laughs, deep and throaty.

Ugh. Panties. Melted.

"Yes, I suppose some things will never change," he allows. His mirth melts into something more … puzzled.

"What?" I ask.

"Nothing," he responds quickly. I give him a look, and he relents. "I just didn't take you for the forward type."

I set the menu back in its holder, then lean toward him. "What type did you take me for?" I'll admit it; the knowledge that he may think we're more than friends has emboldened me.

He leans in closer, only inches away now across the small surface of the table. "The innocent, bashful type, I suppose," he murmurs.

And I can't help it. I burst into laughter. He draws back, watching me curiously.

I wave a hand as I calm myself. "I'm sorry," I

say, catching my breath. "I may be younger than you, but I'm definitely not innocent."

And maybe I do blush a lot around him, but it's not because I'm bashful. But I don't say that part. Because the things being around this man makes me want to do are in no way innocent or bashful, and I don't want to scare him off just when he's come back around.

Nils tips his head. "Exactly how not innocent are we talking here?" he asks in a low voice.

I sink my teeth into my bottom lip. "I don't think that's the kind of thing we should talk about in public. Over lunch."

Nils swallows hard. My insides flutter. But I keep my expression neutral as we stare at each other across the table, the air between us thick with newly blossomed sexual tension.

This. This is exactly what I've craved for so long. That I've dreamed about. That I haven't found in so long. This longing. Attraction like sugar and spice that you can practically taste.

And the thought that he could be feeling it right now, too, is sending tremors of anticipation through my whole body.

The waitress chooses that moment to come over and take our orders, breaking the spell.

I use the opportunity to shift the conversation and ask Nils how he got into managing Francesca Greco's clubs, and if that's something he plans to stick with.

Clearly, he does. Listening to him talk about it, I can *feel* his passion for the job. I've never heard him talk so much, honestly. Though when he asks me why I chose journalism, it reverses the whole dynamic and I tell him how my passion for music, while completely lacking any talent myself, alongside a love of writing, naturally led me to the job.

It isn't until my phone vibrates in my purse that I realize my lunch hour is long since over.

"I'm sorry, I really have to get back to work," I admit sheepishly.

"No, I'm sorry, I should've remembered not everyone runs on nightclub hours," he offers, sliding out of the booth and holding out a hand.

I smile up at him, taking his hand. "Walk me to my car?" I look up into his eyes.

He stares down at me for a moment before nodding silently and tugging me toward the door. He keeps his large, warm hand wrapped around mine as we walk the half-block to where I'm parked.

"This is me," I say, tipping my head at my red Jetta.

He stops and turns toward me, studying my face for a moment. "Thank you for agreeing to see me today," he says.

I smirk up at him, fighting the urge to tease him for taking so damn long to ask. "Thank *you* for lunch. I had a great time," I respond instead.

He nods slowly and a lock of hair falls across his forehead. I fight the urge to reach up and tuck it back in with the rest of his glossy, dark-blond strands. Touching him would be a bad idea right now, because I really do need to get back to work.

"Can I take you to dinner tomorrow?" he asks.

My eyebrows jump in surprise. He's been unreadable until now, but I guess I wasn't the only one feeling this date.

"I'd love that," I admit softly. "Text me?" I squeeze his hand and open the car door.

"I will," he promises. "Goodbye, Alexsis."

My heart flutters at the sound of my name on his lips. "'Bye." I slide into the car and buckle in, fighting the urge to jump back out and into his arms. Instead, I flutter my fingers and blow a kiss at him as I pull away from the curb.

5

NILS

I couldn't get Alexsis out of my mind after our reunion, but now? I'm completely screwed. One hint at our lunch date as to how much there is I don't know about her, a few light touches, the unfulfilled desire to taste her lips, and she's practically turned into an obsession.

How did the adorable little girl of my memories turn into this smart, beautiful creature I can't stop thinking about? I thought perhaps lunch would cool me down; that the reality of her couldn't live up to the temptation that she presented when she appeared in my club. Looking like exactly the kind of woman I'd normally go after with her silky hair, big blue-grey eyes, lush lips, and perky tits accented by a red halter dress that hugged every curve of her delectable little body.

But there's nothing normal about what's going on between Alexsis and me, and as I approach her apartment door, I can only hope she's as mature as she seems. Because I still can't stop thinking that twenty-two … well, it's just so young. Then again, perhaps I'm only thinking of myself at that age, and not giving her enough credit.

I take a deep breath and knock. Even having seen her dressed up before, the sight of her opening the door in a slinky silver dress that ripples over her curves like liquid metal … well, it leaves me speechless, to say the least.

"Hello," she says with a knowing smile. "Don't you look handsome?" Her eyes travel over my black blazer, black button-up open at the collar, and crisp black pants. I'm the night sky to her shining north star. Speechless, indeed.

I clear my throat. "Thank you," I finally manage. "You're absolutely stunning."

Her smile grows as she steps out and closes the door behind her, bringing the smell of jasmine, of sultry night-blooming desire, with her. "Shall we?"

I offer my arm, finally remembering myself. "I hope you're hungry," I murmur, looking down at her.

She stares back up at me, her eyes bright. A sly smile curves her lips. "Starved."

A shiver runs down my spine. Because something about the way she said it made me think she didn't mean for food.

FOOD, IN FACT, HAS BARELY CROSSED MY MIND, EVEN as we dine at one of the hottest restaurants in Los Angeles. The cozy, dark corner we're in has kept the tension going between us by sheer proximity as we eat and talk. And like yesterday, we talk easily and seemingly endlessly.

Unlike yesterday when we discussed our pasts, this time we talk about our lives now. Her career at *Rock Scene* and where she wants to be — a top writer with regular cover bylines. Mine with Baltia — confessing for the first time out loud that I've thought of offering to buy it from Frankie, make it mine completely. Her desire to travel — she surprises me when she shares that she's never traveled internationally. Which, naturally, reminds me of my own world travels and I can't help imagining revisiting my favorites, traveling with her, seeing it through her eyes.

The abruptness of the idea startles even me, so I say nothing. It would be too much, too fast. And yet, staring across the table at her, it feels almost … right.

But then, such is the spell she's weaved over me, leaning close to emphasize a point, reaching for my hand to show connection when I speak … by the end of the meal her body language alone has me so completely enthralled I don't realize that we've been sitting there for hours until the server taps the check presenter and says for the second time, "Whenever you're ready, no rush."

"I believe we've overstayed our welcome," I murmur to her, so he won't hear as he tends to a nearby table.

Alexsis checks her phone. "It is late. I should probably get home anyway," she allows. "Since I have to work tomorrow."

I nod, rising and offering her a hand. As she did yesterday, she takes it without hesitation, but this time I pull her against me as we leave the restaurant.

"As much as I love my job, it must be so nice being able to sleep in," Alexsis laments as I drive her home.

I laugh drily. "Every job has its downsides," I reply.

"What are the downsides for you?" she asks curiously.

I hesitate for a moment, realizing what I'm going to say may sound presumptuous. But then, it is what it is. "You work standard business hours and play on the weekends, right?" She dips her chin in agreement. I can't hide my disappointed frown, despite already knowing the answer. "Even though I'm usually there most of the week by choice, I *have* to be at the club Thursday through Sunday morning. Well, except for sleep, of course."

"Yeah, but you get to see all the performers, too, right?"

I tip my head back and forth as I pull into her apartment complex. "Yes, I guess I do," I accede.

"So, the downside is …?"

I pull into a guest spot in front of her building and turn to her. "I won't get to see you again until Sunday evening," I say more plainly.

I can see the moment she realizes how incompatible our schedules are, and her eyes search mine. "Walk me up?"

I give her a small smile. "Of course."

As we head up the stairs, she stays close, her fingers entwined with mine.

When we reach her door, she slides her hand up

my arm. "So, was that you asking me out again for Sunday?" she teases, smoothing her hand over my lapel.

I reach up and thread my fingers with hers, lifting her hand to my mouth and placing a kiss on her palm. "Yes," I reply simply.

She nods slowly in answer. "Okay. Yes." Her chin tips up and the air is thick with anticipation.

I hesitate. Not because I don't want to kiss her. But because I want to savor this moment. The promise of it. The feeling. The desire.

Her pink lips. Her intoxicating smell. The way ever fiber of me responds to her.

Her mouth opens a fraction, and she sighs. It breaks my restraint, and I pull at her hand while wrapping my other arm around her and drawing her into me. She rises on her tiptoes and pushes her mouth into mine.

Her soft, warm lips open under mine, and I slip my tongue against hers, tasting the wine she had with dinner. I pull her in closer, tipping her head back to give me full access to her mouth as I hold nothing back. I let every desire that has flitted through my mouth play out in our kiss. Her hands slide around my neck and her body presses against mine as the intensity ratchets up.

With the touch of her breasts to my chest, my control slips further, and I ravage her mouth with mine while I run my hands down her lithe body. Our mouths break apart and come back together in a frantic dance of tongues and lips and teeth, and I know if it doesn't stop, I'm going to take her inside and, well, take her. I can't remember the last time I felt this way, and the tenuous grip I have on myself shocks me back to reality.

I slowly withdraw, nipping at her bottom lip gently before letting her go. She gives me a bewildered, lust-fogged look. "You have work in the morning," I explain.

She closes her eyes and sighs. "You're right. I do." She opens her eyes again and smiles. "Thank you for an amazing date, Nils."

I resist the urge to touch her again. To tell her that I hope it's the beginning of many more. I need to get used to the idea first. "Good night, Alexsis," I say instead.

And then, clearly before she can think better of it, she slips inside and closes the door. It takes all of my strength to walk away and get in my car.

THE LIMO PULLS UP AT THE CURB RIGHT ON TIME. I breathe a sigh of relief. As much as I love my job, it's been four days since I've seen Alexsis, and the anticipation has been killing me.

I open the back door, and she peers up at me. My pulse races as we lock eyes, and I extend a hand. She slides hers into mine and steps out.

Her silken sheaf of hair flows over one shoulder. Her lips are an attention-grabbing shade of pink. Her body is on full display in a simple tight, strapless black dress that ends just above her knee. And hot pink stilettos to match her gorgeous mouth. I swallow hard as she joins me, and the car pulls away.

"You sure know how to get a girl somewhere in style," she offers as a greeting.

"And the night has only just begun," I reply, lifting her hand to my mouth and placing a kiss on her palm.

The quick tuck of her lip into her mouth sends a shot of heat into places I can't think about yet.

I keep hold of her hand and lead her to the VIP entrance of Los Jardines.

"Well, aren't you special?" she teases as the bouncers make a path for us and she follows me in.

I pause just inside and smile down at her. "This is another of Frankie's clubs. I managed it for the first year. And while I love Latin music, I just missed Baltia too much. But tonight is Salsa night."

She peers around me, apprehension in her eyes. "Nils, I know I mentioned that I took Salsa classes in college, but that was years ago."

I slip a finger under her chin and draw her gaze up to meet mine. "Don't worry." I wink, then lead her further into the club.

I walk around the back of the crowd, toward the bar, letting her take it all in. What started as Salsa night to try to pull a crowd in on Sundays has now devolved into a night much the same as any for the club. Flashing strobe lights. A packed dance floor. Couples of all kinds grinding to the beat, though there are usually a few serious Salsa couples putting on a show that sets the tone of the evening. It's been a wild success, even if not in the way we intended.

What I'm hoping Alexsis will see is that this isn't some stuffy ballroom dance club for skilled dancers. It's a place to let go and *feel*. The music. The freedom. And hopefully, each other, since we're starting the night on the early side, for clubbing, anyway. I hoped it would take some of the time pressure off, at least.

I order a drink for us both, handing hers off wordlessly. Not that she could hear me now anyway.

She looks up at me. Then down at her drink. And she slugs it back in one go.

I almost laugh. But instead, I master myself. Raising an eyebrow, I do the same and down mine, setting the empty glass on the bar behind me. And I offer my hand.

Alexsis takes it with a grin.

I lead her through the crowd, to the center, where the mass of bodies is thickest. It forces her into my arms immediately. She looks up at me, her hands resting on my chest. Before she has time to let her nerves get the better of her, I start to move.

She follows my steps flawlessly, despite her protests, her feet tracking mine, her hips moving seamlessly with the beat. I press back and spin her out, then draw her back sharply against my chest. Alexsis tips her head back and laughs, and seeing her enjoyment is everything.

Like a cord has been cut, her body loosens, starting to move more fluidly with mine. It's not long before she's turned, her back flush against my front, all notions of "proper" Salsa dancing a distant memory as her ass grinds into me. We move together for a while, getting closer, sweatier, dirtier. She's too sexy. Too enticing. And yet it's too much and not enough all at the same time. She drives me wild, and I'm ready to give in to it.

I skim my hands down her bare arms, wrapping them around her front, pulling her into me. My mouth drops to her ear, testing the waters with a light kiss. She arches, offering the slender column of her neck to me. If I was turned on before, I'm on fire now. But I don't want to make my move here. Like at her apartment before, I have a feeling once we really get started, I'm not going to be able to stop.

As we continue, though, she grinds against me in a way that becomes very hard to ignore. Hard being the operative word. And when she realizes that's exactly what I am, she turns toward me, her eyes locking on mine. It steals the breath from my chest. I can see in her gaze she's determined not to have to stop this time. My whole body tenses with delicious anticipation.

Her arms snake around my neck. Her frame molds to mine. The beat travels through our bodies as one.

I close the small distance between our faces, her breath now hot on my cheeks. I brush my lips lightly over hers. As eager as I am for her, I'm enjoying this.

She sighs, her mouth opening and tilting toward mine. I sink into her, our lips molding together as tightly as our bodies. Chills travel through me as our tongues find each other, as her hands sink into my hair, lightly scratching at my scalp. She tastes of tequila and sin and promise.

I slide my hands down her back, delving deep into her mouth with my tongue, pulling her into me as my fingers skate over the silky skin of her back. Something about it breaks my dam of restraint.

I need this woman. I need to know what she sounds like with my tongue between her thighs. I need to know if it feels as amazing as I imagine to sink into her. I need to know her inside and out, literally and figuratively. But right now? Literally.

When the kiss finally breaks, I lean my forehead against hers, dizzied by our connection. I'm so turned on it's all I can do not to take her right here, right now.

I suddenly understand the time Frankie and Julian practically fucked on the dance floor at Baltia, early in their relationship. Sometimes your need for someone is stronger than your sense of right and wrong.

And I'm ready to do some very wrong things to Alexsis.

I lean in and say loudly enough for her to hear, "Follow me."

And then, with a sharp tug on her hand, I'm leading her through the crowd. Down the hall toward the bathrooms. Then beyond through the employees-only door and toward the management office that I know lies empty beyond. It's probably as far as I can make it, but at least it's not the dance floor in a club owned by the woman I work for.

6

ALEXSIS

My head is still spinning from our kiss when Nils closes the door to the room we just entered and flicks on the lights. It's an office, with a steel desk and leather chair on one side, and a matched leather loveseat on the other.

But I barely have time to take it in before Nils shoves me against the back of the door, the impressive erection I'd felt on the dance floor pushing into my belly as he gazes down at me with lust written all over his face.

Everything in me swoons toward him. God, that kiss. It wasn't just pure fire; it was also filled with potential. Even more than our first. It was more than the lust he's staring at me with now. It was the fulfillment of every girlish fantasy I'd ever held about kissing him.

Though what I feel for him is already far beyond that. I want him so badly it hurts. But there are still things he needs to know before we go there.

"Stop." I say it softly, but he heeds right away, drawing back, brows bunching together.

"What's wrong?" he asks, cupping my cheek and looking earnestly into my eyes.

I swallow hard against a lump in my throat. "There's just so much we haven't talked about. So much we don't know about each other. I can't … *we* can't yet."

His expression darkens. "Who told you?" he asks somberly.

I look up at him quizzically. "Who told me what?"

He stares at me for a moment, his thumb stroking my cheek. "I'm sorry, I thought someone had … You're right. There's much we don't know about each other."

"What did you think someone told me?" I press.

He takes a deep breath in through his nose and slowly lets out a sigh. He steps away, settling down on the loveseat, gesturing for me to join him.

I sit down, now even more disconcerted.

He takes my hand, stroking it. "If it wasn't obvious, I like you Alexsis," he says plainly. "A lot. So, you're right. I think if we want to take this anywhere, I should be completely upfront about myself."

I raise an eyebrow. Because I thought he had been. Or at least more so than anyone I'd met in a long time. "What don't I know, Nils?"

He grimaces. "I didn't want to tell you and change the way you saw me. But I don't want you to feel like I'm holding back. So here it is. After school and before getting into the nightclub business, I was a fashion model. And since you've lived in L.A. your whole life, I'm sure you understand what that lifestyle comes with. Lots of traveling. Lots of partying. Lots of sex. But I promise you, that's all been behind me for years."

I can't help it; a smile breaks over my face. "You thought *that* would change things?" I'm not surprised in the least. He's insanely gorgeous, and I noticed he didn't talk much about what he did before his current job. But I'm no stranger to secrets, so I didn't press.

His expression remains calm, but I'm starting to know him well enough to sense the shift in his emotions. He suddenly seems … uncomfortable? Worried?

"Well, it was quite a lot of sex. I uh …" He clears

his throat anxiously. "I had something of a reputation."

My smile turns into a full-on grin. "Well, that's saying something in this town. What for?"

And Nils actually *blushes*. I bite into my bottom lip, trying not to show how funny I find all of this.

"Orgies?" he says uncertainly. I'm sure he's not uncertain about whether that's what he did, more about telling me. Then he quickly follows it with, "But I'm not an idiot. It was always safe, so I never caught anything. It was just … a lot of orgies." He shifts uncomfortably.

"Nils, you have nothing to worry about. That's not what I was talking about, but I'm glad you told me. More than you know," I admit.

His shoulders drop in relief. "Really?"

I nod. "Really."

"So, you're not scared off?" he asks, squeezing my hand and leaning forward.

"Not even a little. And I hope you're not either. Because I know you see me as young and innocent, but when I said there were things we didn't know about each other, I wasn't talking about you."

Nils's brows shoot up. "What don't *I* know, Alexsis?" he asks, the corner of his mouth tilting up.

And finally, I don't feel scared. Not after his admission.

"I've never told anyone this before," I hedge.

"Your secret is safe with me," he responds reassuringly.

My mouth feels suddenly dry, and I lick my lips, trying to regain enough composure to say out loud what I've never said to anyone.

"I did porn." I scrunch my nose, waiting for his reaction.

Nils stares at me blankly without responding.

After a minute, I swallow hard and clear my throat. "I was an adult film actress," I amend. "To pay for college. I enjoy sex, and I'm not ashamed of that. So, when I was approached to do some high-class videos for a porn site for women, I went for it. It was also all done safely. But yeah. Like I said before, I'm not exactly innocent either." I shrug self-consciously as he continues to stare. There's so much more, but I need to see how he reacts to this first.

And I thought after his admission he'd take it a little better. But his continued silence is unnerving. Guess I was wrong.

"If that's too weird for you, I understand." I slide my hand out from under the dead weight of his. "I'm not embarrassed by it. It's just not something I felt like anyone needed to know. Until now, anyway." I lift a shoulder.

And wait for him to say something. Anything. But he just stares at me.

"Please say something," I urge him.

His mouth opens. Then closes. He shakes his head.

Well, shit.

"Look. I get it, that's big. Maybe too big. I should just … go and give you some time to think about it." I stand up. "I'll … I'll talk to you later, then."

His eyes flick up to me, still clearly stunned. So, I do the only thing I can do in the absence of any sort of response from him. I turn around and leave.

I'm not sad. Just disappointed, I decide, as I reach for the door handle.

That is, until a hand closes over mine, turning me around.

7

NILS

I pull Alexsis to me, staring down at her, still in complete and utter disbelief.

"I'm sorry," I tell her. "I'm just in shock. Don't go."

She looks up at me warily. "It's understandable. Though I thought you might not be quite *so* shocked, considering."

I shake my head. "No, Alexsis," I correct her softly. "I'm shocked at what a fucking idiot I am. That I stayed away from you for months because I didn't want to taint you." I laugh at that thought. God, how wrong can one man be? "All that time wasted." I bring my eyes back to hers. And I see hope in her gaze.

"*That's* why you never called?" she asks incredulously.

I nod. "That's why I never called. I didn't want to corrupt the daughter of the family that took me in." I shake my head and chuckle. "Turns out, we're more well-suited for each other than I thought."

She smirks up at me. "I guess older doesn't mean wiser," she teases.

I lean in, my lips hovering over hers. "No, but it may mean just a touch more experience," I murmur.

I can feel her breathing pick up. "Show me what you've got, old man," she taunts, licking those perfect pink lips of hers.

An uncharacteristic grin spreads over my face as I put her back up against the door. Just where I had her before. But now I know she won't be scared off. That she'll appreciate every dirty thing I want to do to her.

I cage her in, putting my hands on the door on either side of her. I lay a light kiss on her lips.

"First, I think I'll play with your tits," I murmur, licking down the length of her neck and trailing my mouth down to one of her nipples that's protruding through her dress. I bite it none too gently and she gasps and arches into me. I do it to the other for good measure before grasping both breasts through the fabric and kneading them with my hands. Alexsis groans with approval.

"And then?" she asks, panting heavily.

"And then I'm going to eat you out until you come," I promise, dropping to my knees. I press my face into the warm center of her legs, breathing in her scent through the fabric. I feel her fingers lace into my hair, scraping against my scalp.

I lift one of her perfect legs up, her dress shifting just enough to reveal a nude thong soaked through with her arousal. I rest her leg over my shoulder, cupping the back of her leg and ass with one hand, pulling her toward me. I use the other to lift her dress fully so that I can taste her. I slip my tongue between her legs, along the base of the fabric, feeling the trembling heat of her pussy just within reach.

With a growl, I shove her panties aside and dive into her, my tongue pushing its way between her lips, tasting her, priming her, sending her head back, knocking against the door as she moans.

I let the hand holding her backside slip between her cheeks and stroke her ass, seeing how she responds. When she doesn't shy away, I rub a finger over her. Her pussy gets even more soaked, and I know she's ready.

I use the hand holding her to finger her ass while

my tongue drives into and over her pussy. The leg she has on my shoulder starts to shake, her fingers grip my hair, and I know she's close. So, I fuck her harder from both sides. She comes, moaning my name more beautifully than I'd even imagined. And we're just getting started.

I let her leg down slowly and rise, pressing against her and kissing her fiercely. She grabs at my shirt, and I allow her to take it off. Her hands run over my chest as she presses her mouth back to mine, her fingers pinching at my nipples as her tongue laves against my bottom lip. My cock strains against my pants, yearning to be inside of her.

"Now what?" she pants against my lips.

I consider that for a moment. As tempting as it is to fuck her beautiful pink mouth, I can tell she needs me to show her I'm okay with everything she shared. That I'm not afraid. That I'm here for it. And fuck am I here for it.

So much so that I'm more vocal than I've ever been with a lover. Something about her brings it out in me.

"Now I'm going to lay you on that couch and suck every inch of your body until I figure out exactly which parts make you scream the loudest, then fuck you while I suck them," I promise, a thrill chasing through me.

And I do exactly that. Turns out there's a spot where her shoulder meets her neck that makes her so wet I have a hard time keeping it together.

I look down at her, now lying on the small couch as I crouch between her legs, her dress bunched around her waist, so her tits are on display and the small strip of hair over her pussy is visible with her panties pushed to the side. And I'm not sure how I haven't already come at the sight.

She looks up at me with glazed eyes, and it sends shivers through me. I let her watch as I unzip. As I pull out my cock. As I roll a condom on. As I tease her entrance. She tips her head up to watch.

"You like that? You like watching?" I ask.

She bites her lip and nods, breathing heavily but not looking away from where I'm rubbing the tip of my jacketed dick over her clit.

I slide in slowly, pressing a hand on her hip to keep her in place as I fill her.

Once I'm in deep, I lean in and kiss her softly, shifting as I pump slowly. "What's your pleasure, baby?"

"You," she breathes.

I tip my head back as my balls tighten at her answer. I look back down into her eyes.

"And you're mine," I assure her, bracing my arms next to her so I can continue to watch her as I slide slowly in, slowly out.

She writhes under me, her hands skimming my back, down to my ass, then back up again. Her touch sends jolts through me wholly unrelated to the amazing feeling of being inside of her. It spurs me on, and I ramp up my speed. When I start to feel my own orgasm build, I break my mouth from hers and move it to that spot on her shoulder. She groans and grinds against me.

I slide one hand down under her leg, lifting it so I can get to her ass as I fuck her. When I slide a finger into her other hole, she clenches hard.

"You like that?" I ask her.

She nods. "Yes," she breathes. "God, yes. More."

With a smile, I give her more. All of it. Everything. My mouth works her skin. My chest rubs her nipples. My hand rubs her ass. My cock takes her pussy, our joined centers creating friction over her clit. I give in to the tightening deep in my core, letting the building need drive the speed of my thrusts until I'm fucking her thoroughly and fast, the tip of my cock more sensitive with every motion until she clamps down, sending me reeling, my orgasm unfurling quickly in hot bursts as lights pop in my eyes. She holds me hard through her own orgasm until I'm empty, sated, and sure that she is, too.

And as I sink down onto her, our mouths melding and my heart pounding, the feeling of the absolute rightness of being wrapped in her settles over me. My doubts about age, experience, and how I "should" think of this woman are obliterated by the reality of what we are: Perfect for each other.

8

———

ALEXSIS

As the pounding of my heart subsides, the heat of Nils's body over me combines with the bliss from a record-setting orgasm to take me to a new level of relaxed and satiated.

"Nils?" I murmur.

He props himself back up on his arms so he can look down at me.

"Next time I get to suck every inch of your body until I figure out exactly which parts make you scream the loudest, then fuck you while I suck them," I promise.

As I expected it to, Nils's cock twitches inside of me and I tip my head back and laugh.

His mouth descends on the spot on my neck, and he swirls his tongue over it, causing me to take in a sharp breath.

"You're incredible," he moans into my skin. His mouth finds mine again, kissing me only briefly. "I'm looking forward to it. But first …"

He pulls out, removes the condom, then wraps it in some tissue and bins it. As he tucks himself back into his pants, he drops to his knees between my legs. His head leans toward me and I suck in a breath. Is he really going to …?

His tongue finds my pussy again and I moan. Yes, apparently, he is. This time he fingerfucks me while he laps at my clit and tweaks my nipple with his other hand. Even the expected is unexpected with Nils, as every lick, suck, and touch drives me wild in ways I can't say it ever has before.

Maybe it's knowing it's him that's doing it. Maybe it's because of the intense attraction I've always felt toward him, and the special magic that I knew we had the moment we reconnected. Or maybe it's just because he's that skilled. And damn if he isn't pretty much the best at what he's doing that I've ever had before, which is saying a lot.

Because when he goes for the shocker again … holy hell. I've never minded that kind of play before. But tonight is the first time I've understood why it's done. I knew it could make everything feel … *more* but god am I feeling it all, and then some. As a result, the next orgasm hits like a freight train. Hard, long, and it splits me into a million blissed-out pieces.

I watch Nils as he gently withdraws. He's so handsome it hurts. Though everything hurts so good right now. I pull my dress back down and scoot up so he can sit beside me. He loops an arm around me and pulls me into his lap.

"Okay, I have an odd question," he hedges.

I raise an eyebrow and give him a smirk. "I think we're past considering questions odd," I offer.

He chuckles. "Yes, perhaps."

I gesture for him to go on.

"What was your porn name?"

I suppress a smile. It's a question I should've expected. "Tessa Temptation," I tell him. "Why? Are you going to go watch my films?" I tease with a glint in my eye. I'm hoping he does because the idea is a surprisingly huge turn-on.

He cocks an eyebrow back at me. "Only if you watch them with me."

My eyes go wide. Oof. I was wrong. There's an even bigger turn-on. Holy hell.

"It won't bother you watching other people fuck me?" I ask slyly.

And I feel him shift in his pants under me. I burst out laughing again.

"Guess not," I follow up.

Nils cups my face and tilts my head so we've locked gazes. "Part of the orgy appeal was watching other people fuck, Alexsis. I have a feeling we're just getting started on finding all the amazing things we're going to do together. And I don't just mean in the bedroom."

I'm rendered speechless, but it's moot as his mouth finds mine for a soft kiss. It's tender and filled with promise. When I pull back, I'm struck hard by the feeling that he's right. Because a man that I'm this attracted to, that I find this fascinating, who not only accepts my past but is excited about what it means for us? He's my unicorn. The thought is over-whelming, to say the least.

I sigh heavily. "I have the biggest 'I told you so' of my life coming from Max," I murmur.

Nils huffs a laugh. "Oh? Why's that?"

"She told me you were into me. I didn't believe her."

Nils's lips tilt in a smile. "If it makes you feel better, I've got the same coming from Frankie."

"Sounds like we were both wrong."

"I've never been happier to be."

"Me neither." I pause. "Nils?"

"Hmmm?" he returns, sounding sleepy.

"How do you feel about bondage?"

His head snaps up. "I feel like if I were physically capable of it, I'd take you home and tie you up for even asking that question."

I grin widely. "Or I could tie you up."

He groans and tackles me into the couch, his mouth demanding on mine. When he pulls back and looks down at me, his gaze is so intense I can feel myself getting turned on again. Good lord, this man.

"I'm not wasting any more time with you, Alexsis. Whatever you want. I'm yours."

I reach up and stroke his beard. I've always been his on some level. He was my first crush, after all.

"Good to know," I reply, not wanting to give too much away. "But I think I need to recharge myself. How do you feel about pie?"

"If you're talking about the pie shop up the road, then I'm pretty much about to propose right now."

I laugh and he smiles widely. "You strike me as a black pepper cherry pie kind of guy. A spicy twist on a classic," I tease, ignoring the shock of his joking about proposing.

He raises an eyebrow. "Seriously. Marry me."

My breath catches. "Seriously?"

He grins, and it's something I've seen him do so rarely that it dazzles me. "Not really, no," he admits. He leans in and kisses me, then rises, extending a hand. "Ready?"

I look up at him. Am I ready? For pie, yes. For Nils … I know that ready or not, I'm in. I slide my hands into his with a smile.

"Ready."

9

ALEXSIS

"**I** told you so," Max says with a smug grin.

I roll my eyes. "Yeah, yeah, yeah. You were right. Nils was totally into me. Happy?"

Max leans forward and rests a hand on my arm, giving me a pointed look. "Yes. But only because *you* are."

Despite my irritation, I don't even fight the smile that breaks over my face in answer. Because I am happy. At least, about my love life for once, anyway.

"Thanks," I murmur. "I am. He's …" I shudder and sigh, not knowing how to finish that sentence. I mean, I know how I want to finish that sentence, but there's so much about me Max doesn't know that would require explaining. And I love the girl, but she's also a colleague, so that's just not going to happen.

Max chuckles. "I know the feeling," she replies with her own satisfied sigh.

"I know you do," I tease. "Things good with you and West, then?"

"I mean … between *us*? So good," she responds. But something in her voice is off.

"But?" I prompt.

She chews on her lip nervously. "Honestly? The band is in some trouble with the record label. Something about not having the rights to use Violent Mood Swings' name to produce a record and hold a concert?" She shakes her head. "West and the rest of the band are all pretty upset."

"Shit," I curse. "I can see why they would be." The wheels in my head start to turn. "Are they even allowed to do that? Own the name, I mean?"

Max shrugs. "Who knows? They're a huge-ass record label. Maybe they are or maybe they aren't, but they'll probably get away with it either way." She growls in frustration. "God, I wish there was something I could do to help. I hate seeing him like this." I raise an eyebrow at her. "What?" she asks.

I give her a bland look. "Uh, you're a rock journalist?" I point out.

She narrows her eyes at me once she gets my meaning. "I can't write about this, Alexsis. *Total* conflict of interest."

Excitement rises in my chest. "But I can," I point out. "In fact, this might be just what I need to snag a byline."

Max arches an eyebrow. "That … could work. We'd just have to sell Jason on you covering it instead of someone more senior."

"Or maybe we just don't tell him I'm doing it," I suggest.

She fixes me with a look. "You know that's not how it goes around here."

I lift a shoulder. "Sometimes when the rules screw you, you have to say screw the rules."

Max snorts, then gives me an appraising look. "Still after that promotion, huh?"

I draw in a slow, deep breath and nod. "Not that I don't love being your assistant," I hedge. "But I'm ready for more."

Max taps a fingernail on her desk and twists her lips to the side. I already know what she's going to say, but I give her the "spit it out" look.

"It's just … you haven't even been here a year yet," she finally says.

This time I level her with a look because I know

she didn't get promoted until she'd been here a couple years. "Do you think I don't have what it takes?" I ask plainly.

Max leans forward and looks me in the eye. "You know *I* think you have what it takes," she says quietly. "But we both know that's not the only thing you need to get ahead around here."

I scoff. "So, what, I need a penis to be taken seriously?"

Max gives me a wry smile. "Well, I can't honestly say that doesn't make a difference," she admits, her eyes darting around, making sure nobody is listening. "But you also know Jason values 'paying your dues.'"

I roll my eyes. "Whatever that means. Talent is talent. If I can bring him an article that sells mags, that should be all that matters."

Max leans back in her chair and sighs. "I mean … I can't say it won't work. But there's more to it than that." She pauses. "I think you just need to be patient."

I clench my jaw against a snarky retort. I know Max is just trying to help. But I didn't get a degree in journalism to be a gofer for years before getting my own byline.

I also don't throw it in her face that I did at least

half of the legwork and writing for the piece on West's apology tour that brought record numbers of new subscribers. Mostly since it was such a difficult situation for her. And really, it was a great chance for me to prove myself. Except, I ended up getting so little credit that it made me realize doing anything as Max's assistant wasn't a recipe for long-term success. Or short-term success even, apparently.

"I hear you," I finally respond, nodding.

She eyes me warily. "Do you?" she asks. "Because I'd hate to see you go off and do something that blew up in your face and got you fired or something."

Reflexively, I give her a sharp look back. I wonder for a moment if she's worried about me or if she's really just worried about being upstaged. And then I feel a little like an asshole, because I know Max wouldn't begrudge me success. At least not consciously. But clearly, she's not behind my plan, so I decide keeping my mouth shut about it is probably for the best.

And then, of course, doing it anyway.

I give her a sweet smile. "You're right. I wouldn't want to risk that," I reply.

Do I respect Max for her talent and success? Absolutely. But we're very different people. She prefers to play by the rules. And I'm more the "no guts, no glory" type.

Nils texts me that Frankie's asked him to check in on her new club and he wants me to join him. Given that our last club date involved some seriously sexy dancing followed by fantastic sex … well, how could I refuse?

Though he asked that I meet him there, he sent a car again at least. I sit in the backseat of said car as it winds through the streets of Hollywood. I run my hands over the buttery leather somewhat nervously. Mostly because I don't know exactly what this is. A date? Work, for Nils anyway? I guess I'll have to take my cues from him, I'm just used to knowing which version of myself I need to be. Or more accurately, whether I need to suppress my inner freak or not.

When we pull up to the club, I slide out to find Nils waiting for me, a hand extended to help me out of the car. I take it and look up at him with a smile as I adjust my purple minidress. His eyes slide over me approvingly and he lifts my hand to his mouth, placing a kiss on my knuckles.

And then he pulls me flush against him, ravishing my mouth. But it's over as abruptly as it began.

"I missed you," he says, nuzzling against my ear, his husky voice sending chills down my side.

I run my hand up his chest and lightly scratch my nails over the back of his neck. "I missed you, too," I murmur, looking up into his eyes.

He steps back, sliding his hand over mine and tugging me toward the VIP entrance. "Come with me," he commands.

I grin. "Yes, sir."

He looks over his shoulder at me and laughs, shaking his head.

Once we're in, I can't contain my curiosity any longer. "So, what are you checking on, exactly?" I shout into his ear, hoping he can hear me over the pounding EDM.

He shrugs and puts his mouth to my ear. "Everything." He leans back and gives me a wink before leading me to the bar.

He orders and hands me a drink a minute later. I give him a quizzical look at his not having one. He shakes his head in response. So, I guess he's not drinking? I shrug and take a sip of mine. Mint and citrus and sugar wrap around my tongue. A mojito. A pretty damn good one.

He points at the drink and raises an eyebrow in question. I give him a thumbs up and try not to smirk at the fact that he ordered a drink that bartenders notoriously hate making. Which he must know, given his line of work. So clearly, he's here to start some shit.

Next, he leads me on a lap around the club, observing the crowds, the DJ, and the atmosphere until we head up a flight of stairs. There's a bouncer at the top who Nils fist bumps. The dude then lets us into what is clearly the VIP area.

Just as we've barely cleared the entrance, a curvy blonde in black leather pants and a red halter approaches Nils.

I narrow my eyes as she leans into him and puts a hand to his chest while she speaks into his ear. When she pulls back, he nods and the blonde walks past us and down the stairs without even acknowledging my presence.

I turn and give Nils a sharp look. He chuckles and pulls me against him.

"That was Emma, the manager. It's her first week in the role, and Frankie wanted me to check in on her." I flush a little in embarrassment and nod my understanding. Nils clearly doesn't miss a thing because he leans in again and whispers in my ear, "Were you jealous?"

I have to think about that for a moment. Not out of reluctance to admit it, but because I didn't even recognize that was the feeling her touching him had evoked. But yes, I realize it was. I look back up at him and nod.

His eyes bore into mine as his hand tightens on my backside. We stare at each other and the heat in his eyes matches the heat between my thighs. Apparently, feeling jealous is a bit of a turn on for me. And possibly for him, too.

He leans in slowly and nips gently at my lips before withdrawing and leading me to the railing. Back in observation mode, Nils's eyes scan the crowd for a few minutes. And while he watches them, I sneak furtive glances at him.

He finally catches me and one of his rare smiles nearly bowls me over. He snakes an arm around my waist and pulls me close. "Follow me," he murmurs into my ear.

He turns and heads deeper into the VIP section, down a dark hall. We pass restrooms, then a surveillance room, then round a corner.

"What, no dancing first?" I tease him as he comes to a door labeled "office."

He shoots me a wicked look over his shoulder as he opens the door and pulls me inside. "Later," he promises, leading me to the desk. He sits down on the edge and pulls me between his legs, nuzzling into my neck. "Your scent has been driving me crazy since you stepped out of the car." His tongue licks up the front of my throat and my fingers slide into his hair, tugging as the sensations he's causing in me curl through my body.

I take a step back, putting some space between us. "Oh really?" I tease, trailing a finger down his chest as I walk around the desk. I turn to face him from the opposite side. "What are you going to do about it?"

Nils braces on the desk, his hand gripping the edge and he *growls*. A sly grin spreads over my face at the possessive noise. I lean down over the desk, shaking my hips in invitation.

In a flash, he's rounded the desk and lifted the hem of my dress, sliding his hands over my sex. I lay my head down on the desk and look back at him, licking my lips.

"You gonna fuck me right here, you naughty boy?" I taunt him. He sucks in a sharp breath and hisses it back out. But his only response is to unbuckle his belt. My body tightens in anticipation.

"That's right, no foreplay, baby. You know you need this pussy *right now*."

Nils rolls a condom on and again answers with his actions, slamming into me. I gasp as I slide up the desk, as he stretches and fills me. But he doesn't wait for me to adjust, he simply unleashes. I close my eyes to focus on the pleasure, groaning with each punishing thrust, unable to so much as move to meet him.

"Alexsis," he grits out. My eyes fly open to meet his. "Keep those eyes open while I fuck you, naughty girl."

I bite into my lip and nod, a fresh wave of arousal making me even slicker and tighter under his delicious assault.

"Use that pussy, baby," I encourage him.

"Yeah? You like it when I fuck that pussy hard enough to milk my cock?" he says, low and out of breath.

I try to arch, but all it does is push him deeper and I gasp.

God, the dirty talk. I've always been mouthy during sex, but hearing Nils do it? Unexpected. Thrilling. Ecstasy.

"I love it," I admit once I'm able to speak again. "I love you fucking me hard and deep. I love hearing you talk dirty while you use my hole. Let me hear you come because of my pussy, baby."

Nils's thrusts stutter at my words before picking up even harder and faster. "Touch yourself, Alexsis," he commands. "I need you to come and —"

"Oh shit!" someone exclaims.

My head snaps up to see the blonde — Emma — in the doorway. Apparently, we were fucking and dirty talking too loudly to hear the door.

She gapes at us for a moment while Nils slows … but doesn't stop. A feral grin spreads over my face.

"Sorry, you can't join in," I say, not sounding sorry at all. "But feel free to stay and watch."

Nils lets out a dark laugh and picks up his pace again.

"Are you fucking kidding me?" Emma demands. "You can't be … This is so … Stop it!"

I set my head back down on the desk, determined to ignore her. I reach down and finger my clit. I was so close anyway that even the slight brush sends me reeling and my walls clamp down on Nils's dick.

"Oh fuck, Alexsis," he groans, thickening inside of me as he comes. The sound and feel of his orgasm heightens my own and I groan with him.

Emma lets out a disgusted noise and flees the room, the sounds of our orgasms chasing after her.

Nils smacks me hard on the ass as he pulls out. "Well, that was interesting."

I rise, shimmying my dress back into place before turning and looking up at him. "That was fucking hot," I correct him.

Nils smirks down at me. "It was," he agrees. "Still, I think we should go to my place before Emma has another conniption."

"No dancing?" I pout teasingly.

He leans in, lust clear in his glazed eyes. "Not tonight. But don't worry. I'm far from done with you, naughty girl."

I shudder in anticipation. "Then lead the way."

MULTIPLE ORGASMS LATER, NILS AND I COLLAPSE together in his low, black satin-sheeted bed. I'm pleasantly sore *everywhere* and not sad at all that we didn't get to dance. In the club, anyway. There was plenty of dancing — and dirty talk — between the sheets.

"Had enough, naughty girl?" Nils murmurs, running his fingers down my back.

I snort and turn to look at him. "You're not seriously suggesting you can go again right now?"

He smiles vaguely. "I don't need an erection to fuck you."

My breath catches at his words, and I press my lips to his. "Even I need a break sometimes," I admit.

He chuckles lowly. "Mmm." He slides down, molding his body to mine. "I suppose I do, too. But something about you has made me … insatiable." He kisses my neck, and I tip my head back to give him better access, relishing in his touches, even if my libido is sated for the moment.

"It's been a long time since I've had a lover who could keep up," I admit. "I'm impressed."

Nils props his head up on his hand and looks down at me. "Be with me, Alexsis," he murmurs in a serious tone.

The abruptness of his comment has my eyes snapping open. "I *am* with you, Nils," I point out.

His brow furrows. "No, I mean, be with *just* me. I don't want to just claim your body."

Something inside me simultaneously melts and hardens. I realize it's the very thing he's asking for: my heart.

"Are you asking me to be your girlfriend?" I respond quietly.

"Something like that," he agrees.

I raise an eyebrow. "Something *like* that or *that*?" I press.

He lifts a shoulder. "I dislike that word but ... yes, in essence."

I press my lips together. "Here's the thing ..." I take a deep breath and close my eyes for a moment. When I reopen them, his eyes have tightened with concern. "I want to be honest with you, Nils. And that's big for me. Because I feel like there are two sides of me ... the side I have to show to the world, and the real me. And those sides? Well, they have *very* different love lives."

Nils is silent for a minute before he finally says, "I don't know what that means."

I rub my lips together and sit up. He follows suit.

"It means, I've had boyfriends — men I've exclusively dated. But I've *never* promised sexual exclusivity. Ever. Romantic? Sure. I can do that. But sexual? I ... I just need more. I have things I do that I love that I'd have to stop doing."

Nils leans back into the headboard, slinging one arm behind his head for support. I try not to stare at how it makes the lean muscles of his bicep pop.

"So, these boyfriends ... you don't tell them about your other activities?" he asks thoughtfully.

"No," I admit. "But I don't lie about them either."

"Not telling *is* lying," he replies, clearly understanding what I'd meant.

I inhale deeply and let it out. "Yeah, I guess. But …" I trail off and shake my head. Nils tilts his to the side and fixes me with a questioning look. I let out another sigh and look up at the ceiling. Knowing I'm an asshole for what I'm about to say. "I've never wanted to be with someone enough to stop having sex with other people. I'm not sure I'm capable of it."

Nils rests a hand on my knee, stroking gently. The motion makes me look down at where his fingers brush my skin. What I don't say is that I thought Nils might be the one to break that mold … until he asked me to be with him. And only him.

"So, these other people … it's just sex?" he asks.

My eyes lift to meet his. "Yes."

He cocks an eyebrow. "And you have no intimate feelings beyond the physical with those lovers?" I let out an ironic laugh and his brows bunch together. "Why is that funny?"

"Would you be asking me that question if I were a man?" I point out.

Nils raises an eyebrow. "Yes, actually I would. I have."

Now my eyebrows fly up. "You've been in relationships with men?"

"Yes." His straightforward answer shouldn't surprise me, but for some reason, it does. "You haven't been in relationships with women?" he asks.

I shake my head. "Just sex," I say. "I'm pansexual, but no, I've never been in a romantic relationship with a woman." I shrug.

"Ah," he replies succinctly. "But you're still young." He looks down and I sense his mood shift. "It's only natural for you to want to continue exploring your sexual and romantic options."

I almost groan in frustration. "What do you identify as?" I parry back. Nils looks back at me in confusion. "Pan? Bi? Omni?"

"I've never labeled it," he responds thoughtfully. "But then, where I was raised, we don't have the kind of stigma attached to sexuality that exists here."

"Okay … my point was going to be that whatever you label it, age isn't prescriptive of sexual appetite. I have a high sex drive. I have since I hit puberty. I have no reason to believe that will change until and unless it actually does. So, I'm not writing off romance and relationships, just monogamy. In my opinion, it's the opposite of being young and immature to be one-hundred percent honest about that," I insist vehemently.

Nils looks like he's fighting a smile. "I suppose you're right."

I can't decide whether I should glare at him or kiss him. Either way, he's definitely got me all riled up. The thought deflates me a little. "I'm sorry. You asked a simple question, and I gave you a fairly complicated answer with more than a little snark."

Nils's fingers tug at my chin, drawing my gaze to his. "You gave me an honest answer and shared parts of you I know you don't share lightly," he replies. "Thank you."

I nuzzle my cheek into his palm, my face warming at his response. "You're welcome."

"So romantically monogamous, but not physically? Those are your terms?" he summarizes. I dip my chin in agreement and his eyes tighten. "Does that go both ways? Because you let me fuck you like a doll over that desk because you were jealous of Emma barely touching me."

My jaw drops at his blunt — and totally accurate — statement.

I think about his question deeply for a moment. He's not wrong — I was irrationally and uncharacteristically jealous.

But still, the thought of fucking other people with Nils … a pleasant shudder runs through me.

"I didn't know what she was or wasn't to you," I finally respond, meeting his curious gaze. "And in the future, I'll try not to react before you can explain."

Nils surveys me carefully. "And I'll do the same. But any sex that's not just us will clearly merit careful discussion." He purses his lips, concern written all over his face.

Still, hope sparks in my chest that maybe, just maybe, I've finally found someone who understands. Who can meet my needs in a partner.

"Of course. And there'd be no sex outside of us without agreeing to it beforehand," I add. Nils's expression shifts and he withdraws his hand from my knee. "What?" I reach for his hand, unnerved. When he wraps his hand around mine, it settles me slightly.

"You said 'outside of us'" he points out. "Which I take to mean you plan to have sex with someone else without me there." He doesn't meet my eyes.

And the nerves return. Because normally? That's exactly how I'd play it with someone I'd just started dating. Take it at the pace it goes and get my immediate sexual needs fulfilled elsewhere until we were officially sexually exclusive — not that the latter happens often or lasts long.

But my relationship with Nils — because clearly that's what this is now — is new territory.

"I don't know," I admit. "I mean, usually, yes, that's how it'd go down. But this isn't normally how things play out." I press my lips together, knowing he needs reassurance right now that I'm into him, but not knowing how to give it. Because honestly, most guys just can't keep up. And while I hope Nils can, there's every chance it won't work out for that or other reasons. "Can't we just take this day by day?"

His gaze finally lifts to meet mine. I see concern there, but I also see heat. I crawl into his lap, straddling him. He inhales sharply and I rub my sex over his cock.

"Please?" I ask, mock pouting.

The corner of his mouth tilts up, and he pinches my bottom lip with his thumb.

"I think that's best," he finally agrees. And then seals it with a kiss. And an orgasm.

10

———

NILS

Frankie calls me into the club early on Saturday, forcing me out of bed long before I'd normally be up. So I'm already not in the best mood when I stroll into her office to find her, Julian, and Emma seated around the room.

I raise an eyebrow as I take the open seat next to Emma across from Frankie. Julian leans on the credenza behind her, his arms folded over his massive chest, his face unreadable, as usual.

Silence ripples through the room for a moment before Frankie leans back in her chair.

"Thanks for joining us," she opens.

I remain impassive, knowing Frankie either wants a report on Allure in front of Emma or …

Emma tattled on me to Frankie after catching Alexsis and me fucking.

After another beat of silence, it's Julian who breaks first. "So, you gonna tell us what this is all about or what?" he asks, his eyes fixed on Emma.

Emma's chin tips up as she studiously avoids looking at me.

Ah. The latter. Though she hasn't tattled yet … but obviously she's about to.

I can't help the smirk that spreads over my lips, of which Frankie takes note, and lifts an eyebrow.

"Nils paid Allure a visit on Thursday," Emma opens, then pauses, shooting me a dirty look.

Frankie's raised eyebrow turns on Emma. "Which I asked him to do. I wanted a report on how you're doing."

Emma looks a little affronted at the idea of Frankie checking up on her, and my smirk deepens. Though I shouldn't be so smug; the tension that Emma has directed at me right now isn't going to make it easy for Frankie to navigate her loyalties.

"Fine, okay, I guess I get that," Emma finally allows. "But it's even worse that he was supposed to be working because I caught him balls deep in some skank on the desk in my office."

The corners of Frankie's mouth tighten, and I'd

swear she was about to smile. "Well, that *is* a bit unprofessional," she replies tightly. Julian snickers behind her.

My eyes flick up to his and he smiles blithely at me. Because we all three know that Frankie and Julian fuck on this desk every Sunday afternoon. At least, that's the only regular time I've been able to pick out. There are still the occasional other times, but given their new penchant for routine, I've learned to listen at the door for a moment before I knock or, heaven forbid, walk in uninvited.

Not that it bothers me in the least. It's her desk. Her office. Her club. But I don't own Allure, nor is it my primary responsibility, so I can see in hindsight how it was a slight to Emma. Though it was hard to think about that in the moment.

"Am I missing something?" Emma asks, noting the look passing between Julian and me.

Frankie sighs and gives her friend a pitying look before turning her gaze to me. "Alexsis?" she asks. I nod. She presses her lips together. "I'm really trying to fight the urge to fist-bump you right now."

"Frankie!" Emma gasps in surprise. Julian chuckles.

Frankie turns back to Emma. "Look. I get it. I'm sure it was very shocking for you," she says soothingly, then turns her gaze at me. "And for the love of god, Nils, try to use a little discretion and fuck somewhere else next time?" I dip my chin in agreement as I fight a smile. She turns back to Emma. "But seriously, I thought you were going to accuse Nils of something way, way worse than that. I mean, that's not to say it wasn't inappropriate but I'm going to be honest with you, Emma. We've all fucked in every damn club I own. I don't know what to tell you. It's generally not a discipline-worthy event, so long as it's not on the clock or in public spaces. And it's definitely something you could have told me privately." *So as not to embarrass yourself like this* hangs in the air as Emma turns bright red.

"So, you're saying what he did was okay? What if another employee had caught them? God, what if a *patron* had caught them?" Emma insists.

"You know the offices are off-limits to everyone but management," Frankie points out.

"That's beside the point," Emma retorts.

Frankie taps her nails on the arm of her chair. "Fine. Will you please give us a moment alone with Nils?" Frankie replies.

"You're not just going to let him off the hook, are you?" she asks sharply.

"No, we're not going to let him off the hook," Julian assures her.

Emma scrutinizes both Julian and Frankie for a moment before deciding to accept that. Then, with a nod, she rises, shooting me an angry look on her way out.

As the door snicks shut behind her, I let out the breath I'd been holding and meet Frankie's amused stare.

"Truly, I'm sorry for upsetting Emma," I tell her sincerely, heading off whatever admonishment was coming.

Frankie snorts. "While I appreciate that, her making a mountain out of this molehill has more to do with her than you," she assures me. "But that being said, you still shouldn't have fucked someone in what's mostly her office."

I put on my best penitent expression. "I know. It's no excuse, but I wasn't exactly thinking clearly when it happened."

Julian smirks. "It isn't an excuse. But … we get it."

Frankie shoots him a suggestive look, and he winks at her. When she turns back to me, her cheeks are tinged pink. "Anyway, it was timely, because I'd already intended to share something with you that, coincidentally, will fix this particular problem," she continues as she opens a drawer, retrieves something, and tosses it over the desk to me.

I snatch it from the air and open my palm to find two small keys on a ring. I look up with a questioning look.

"I just finished moving the stuff from the storage room down the hall into an offsite unit," Julian explains.

"We're giving you your own office," Frankie adds in response to my bewildered look. "No more borrowing mine when I'm not here."

I look between them, shocked. Since I bounced between clubs so regularly, it had never bothered me to use the existing offices. But their doing this is a gesture I hadn't expected. One that goes deeper than four walls, a ceiling, and a floor. Frankie's eyes glow with the same appreciation I'm feeling right now.

"So, my punishment is —"

"From now on you are required to fuck in your office and your office only, young man," Frankie says mock-sternly with a teasing grin. "We're moving furniture in tomorrow after ..." She trails off and bites her lip. But I know what she was going to say. After she and Julian fuck in *her* office.

I laugh and shake my head. "Thank you," I say simply, rising to leave.

"Nils?" I turn back at Frankie's call. "I'm happy for you."

My eyes bounce between her and Julian, and she gets my meaning. I'm happy for her, too. In a way I don't feel like I was ever fully capable of until now. Until Alexsis.

The first thing I do when I leave Frankie's office is text Alexsis that I want to see her tomorrow night. I have an office to christen, and just the idea already has me semi-hard.

But the next thing I do is take a deep breath and calm myself, then head into the club to find Emma and smooth things over.

11

———

ALEXSIS

"You know, Jim and Janie Roderick's son is here for the weekend," Dad says carefully casual, as we filter out of Sunday morning church service. "He's living out near you now."

I stifle a laugh. "Jonathan? Dad, he's three years younger than me," I remind him with a soft smile.

"Well, sure, but he's going to school out there for … something science-y," Dad returns with a shrug. "He's a real bright kid. I bet you two would have a lot in common, what with living in the same area now and all."

Asher snorts behind me and then covers it with a cough. My mother pats him on the back gently, oblivious to his attempts at hiding his laughter. Aiden smirks at me and I beam back in a way that makes it clear I'll take the heat for now, but they'll get theirs soon enough.

"Oh look, there they are now," Dad says happily as we exit the chapel.

"Just tell him you're seeing someone," Aiden mutters as Dad makes a beeline for the Rodericks.

I shoot him a swift look. "I will if you do," I taunt quietly under my breath.

Aiden's eyebrow ticks, but he says nothing. I give him another smug smile.

Which is promptly wiped off my face as Dad returns with Jonathan in tow, and I'm forced to make small talk under the intense late-morning sun.

It's awkward, and not just because I'm sweating in my long-sleeved blouse and full-length skirt. I remember Jonathan from high school, and he's every bit the geeky, enthusiastic kid he was the last time I saw him four years ago. Albeit a bit taller.

Thankfully, he turns down Dad's invitation to lunch, but not before we're coerced into exchanging phone numbers.

I breathe a sigh of relief as we head back to the van, and Aiden falls into place beside me again.

"So does that mean you're actually seeing someone?" he murmurs quietly, trying and failing not to look interested.

"Maybe," I reply airily. "How's Josh?"

"He's good. Now shush," he mutters, tensing a bit at the mention of his boyfriend. His eyes flick to Dad holding the van door open for Mom. We slide into the back wordlessly.

I feel a bit like an asshole for putting Aiden on edge because seeing my brothers is one of the main reasons I come here every Sunday. Even though they both live nearby, we all have jobs and lives. So normally I look forward to the visit, nagging from my parents to get married and start making babies aside.

Dad's attempt at setting me up was totally predictable. As was Aiden's teasing. But where I would normally laugh it off … well, I find I'm irritated, and it takes me until we've sat down for lunch to figure out why.

As Dad questions my brothers about their weeks — work, their love lives, their hobbies, their love lives, whether they prayed every day this week, their love lives — it hits me.

I'm so used to telling my parents nothing real about my life. How could I? It would break their hearts. And it would mean tearing apart our family.

It's why I've always looked for guys I could bring home to placate my parents with. And even with that intent, I never really found one. But now I've found someone I *am* excited to be with. And there's no way in hell I can say a word. It's the first time I've ever been disappointed with having to deceive them.

Like he hears my thoughts, Aiden's eyes flick to me. Until Asher clears his throat, and all eyes turn to him.

"So, I have something to tell everyone," he says, clearly nervous. He wrings his hands. "Katie and I are engaged."

In any other family, that news would've been met with cheers and congratulations. It's what I feel like doing. I've only met Katie twice, but I like her for Asher. Unfortunately, all eyes now move to Dad.

And Dad's eyes meet Mom's. I can see the disappointment on both of their faces and my heart breaks for my brother.

"Well, son," Dad finally manages. "That's … big news." He pauses and you could hear a pin drop in the room. "Are you sure though? No need to rush these things."

And there it is. No need to rush marrying someone they *don't* approve of, though by all means, rush to marry someone they *do*.

Asher noticeably deflates, and my chest aches with the desire to hug him.

"Yeah, Dad, I'm sure," he responds dully. "We've been dating for four years. I love her. Aren't you happy for me?"

Mom reaches out and squeezes Asher's hand with a reassuring smile. "Of course we're happy for you, dear."

Surprisingly, Dad doesn't contradict her, but he doesn't answer either. He simply goes back to eating, making his displeasure obvious to everyone. Because, while always polite, Dad has never made a secret of the fact that he expects Asher — all of us, really — to marry within our religion. Well, his religion. It's debatable whether any of his children claim it as theirs. Either way, Katie isn't Mormon. She's not even Christian, actually. And while it's not against our teachings to marry outside of the faith … well, Dad's old school.

So, when Asher ignores Dad and leans over to receive Mom's hug, I know he hadn't expected any better anyway.

I leap up and round the table to give Asher my own hug, finally.

"Congratulations," I murmur as I embrace him. "I'm so happy for you guys."

He gives me a half-hearted smile when he pulls away. "Thanks, Sis."

Aiden follows, and Mom starts asking questions about the wedding that make Dad draw further in. And what should've been happy news has cast a pall over the room until Dad finally can't take it anymore.

Aiden notices that Dad is about to start in on Asher again almost as soon as I do. "So, you guys won't believe who I heard from," he pipes up.

Asher gives him a relieved look. "Who?"

"Nils Larssen!" Aiden responds enthusiastically.

And my heart drops. "What?" I ask.

"I'm actually a little disappointed in you, Alexsis. He emailed me a couple of months ago and said he ran into you," he replies, clearly oblivious to my internal panic.

"Sorry, must've slipped my mind." The lie rolls easily off my tongue despite my brain trying to piece together what the hell is going on. "But if he emailed you two months ago, why didn't you say something sooner?"

Aiden shrugs. "It's an old email address I don't check often," he offers. "But cool, right? I can't believe you ran into him." He looks up. "Apparently, he's still living here and has been managing night-clubs in Hollywood."

"Wow, that's awesome," Asher says.

"Yes, isn't that something," Mom says with a smile. "I had no idea he was still in the States. How lovely. You should invite him to join us for lunch sometime soon."

Sheer panic overtakes me. I've worked so hard to keep so much from my family. And this thing with Nils is so new. I cannot let these worlds collide. Not yet. Probably not ever.

But I also can't say a damned word.

"Totally. It'll be just like old times," Aiden says with a grin. Then turns on me. "Remember how you used to have such a huge crush on him, Alexsis?"

My answering laugh is feeble and forced. "Yeah, that was hilarious," I reply tensely.

My family continues to reminisce about Nils, and bands of iron snake around my chest as everything spins out of my control.

12

NILS

I'm running a hand over my sleek new desk when Alexsis appears in the doorway. I jump up, surprised.

"Alexsis, I didn't expect you so soon," I offer, rounding the desk to embrace her. "How'd you get in?" I'd thought I was alone in the club and am suddenly concerned I'd forgotten to lock up.

"Frankie was on her way out and let me in," she replies.

I slide my arms around her and lean in to kiss her, but there's a tension in her expression, her body that stops me short. "Is everything okay?"

Her eyes bounce between mine as if she's debating what she wants to say.

"Fine," she finally says tightly. Clearly not fine. She gestures around. "So, what's all this?"

I study her face for a moment longer. "My new office. What do you think?" I step back and survey the half-placed furniture and boxes. "About its potential, I mean. I know it still needs some work."

She huffs a short laugh. "It's great. Congratulations."

I step back into her and cup her face in my hands. I'm unsure what to say since she's already denied anything being wrong. "I'd hoped you'd help me christen it," I finally murmur.

She closes her eyes and breathes deeply. When she reopens them, there's a clarity and fire in her gaze that wasn't there before. "That's exactly what I need," she breathes.

"Is it?" I question.

She pushes me around the desk until the backs of my legs hit the chair. "Yes. Now sit, bitch."

I raise an eyebrow and sink into the seat. "Yes, mistress," I tease, running my hands up her legs, lifting her skirt. I raise an eyebrow and meet her eyes. "No panties?"

She shakes her head and leans in to rub her hand over my cock through my pants. "No. Now take your cock out like a good boy."

It's a command I can't refuse. And once I do, we're fucking before I even know what's happening, her taking charge and riding me like her life depends on it.

It's simultaneously mind-blowing and worrisome. Because I've felt the need that has seized Alexsis right now; the need to take back control when something else in your life is spiraling away from you.

As we share a climax, I can only hope she'll also eventually share what's bothering her.

Before she's even caught her breath, she's looking down at me intensely. "There's somewhere I want to take you."

I raise an eyebrow. "Are you sure tonight is the best night?" I ask, alluding to her state of mind.

Her expression tightens. "If you don't want to, you can just say no," she says shortly, climbing off of me.

"It's hard to give an answer when I don't know what I'm agreeing to," I respond, watching her shimmy her skirt back down.

"It's where I go to get what I need. And it's something you should probably experience before you decide whether you're really in this or not."

My jaw clenches against the response that forms on my tongue. I'm not a fan of this aggressive and slightly combative version of her, but I bite that thought back as I pull off and discard the condom, then right my clothes. She watches me until I'm done. I rise and stand over her.

"You still haven't said where we're going," I point out evenly.

She runs her hands up my chest, lacing them around my neck and pressing herself into me. "It's a sex club, Nils," she says in a sultry voice, looking up at me from under her eyelashes. "Think you can handle that?"

I huff a laugh. "Yes."

WE DRIVE IN SILENCE, BUT I CAN TELL SOME OF THE fight has drained out of her when she threads her fingers with mine as she gives me directions. I breathe a sigh of relief. If we're going to do this, I'd much rather it be with more positive feelings around the experience. Though I realize that I'd go, regardless. If she needs this to deal with whatever's on her mind … well, either way I plan to show her I can handle this side of her.

When we park, she goes to get out, but I stop her with a hand on her thigh. "What are we doing, Alexsis?" I ask quietly.

She sighs. "We're here to fuck, Nils," she says touchily.

The corner of my lips tugs up. "I figured that much," I reply, spearing her with a look. "I suppose I should've phrased that differently. What are we *not* doing?"

"Ah," she murmurs, nodding. "I hadn't thought that far ahead."

I give her a small, indulgent smile, sliding my hand between her legs and under her skirt. Lightly stroking her pussy. "Am I the only one fucking you tonight?" I murmur as her hips shift.

She shoots me a deeply frustrated look as I continue to lightly stroke her. "Do you want to watch someone fuck me?" she breathes.

A chuckle escapes me. "That depends on what I'm doing while you're being fucked. And by whom. Did you have someone in mind, naughty girl?" I circle my finger around her clit.

She sucks in a breath and groans. "There's a guy — Brody, the owner's son — he's almost always around," she breathes.

I nod slowly. "And he fucks you well?" I demand.

Her hand covers mine, and she pushes down until my fingers slide into her dripping-wet pussy before nodding. "Yes, but not as well as you." Her eyes are glazed when they meet mine.

"Anyone else you'd want to involve? Another man? Woman?"

Her eyes snap to mine, narrowed and full of fire. "No," she replies hotly. "No other women."

I curl my fingers inside of her with a smile. I may be more romantically possessive over Alexsis, but clearly she's more physically possessive over me. Interesting.

I pull her hand into my lap and over my thickening cock to show her how that makes me feel.

"Then let's go," I reply simply.

I follow Alexsis in and it's not my first visit to a sex club, so I'm not surprised by the low lights and naked, writhing bodies everywhere as soon as we get past the inner doors. But Alexsis leads us beyond all that, down a hall, past multiple doors, all in different colors.

I'm intrigued when she stops at a purple door and knocks four times.

When the door swings open, a naked, leggy brunette grins at Alexsis.

"Tessa," the brunette purrs at Alexsis, beckoning her forward. Then her dark eyes flick to me, wandering over my face, then down my body. "And you brought a friend." Her voice is filled with lustful approval. I remain impassive, waiting to see what else is in store beyond.

The room is lit with purple down lights, and matched plush benches lined along one wall with all manner of pillows. The far wall is covered with pegs and shelves that contain every sex toy imaginable. A large, purple satin-sheeted bed sits on the other side of the room. And on it is a naked young man, surrounded by three other naked women.

The guy is rolling a condom on as he watches the women play with each other; one eating out another, the third suckling at the breasts of the woman being serviced. Her moans bounce off the walls. The fourth woman rejoins them, positioning her ass toward the guy so he can fingerfuck her.

It's more debauchery and flesh and sex than I've seen at once in quite a while, and my cock aches behind my zipper. The smell of scented lube hangs in the air, and suddenly I feel ten years younger. Like my early-twenties self who fucked his way through half of Los Angeles.

Alexsis looks up at me like she knows, a smirk playing about her perfect mouth.

The young man, Brody, presumably, rises to his

knees as we approach, sinking into the brunette with a groan. His eyes flick up to meet Alexsis's.

"Tessa," he says, echoing the brunette's greeting. "We've missed you. Why don't you introduce us to your friend and join us."

But Alexsis's gaze turns to me. I see her hesitation, and I instinctively know she's nervous that I'll want to touch these women. I place a hand on her back reassuringly. I lean in and murmur in her ear, "I'm here for you. Only you. He can fuck you while I watch, or I can fuck you while he watches. Whatever you want. But I'm not touching anyone except you." Her back arches slightly under my hand and she nods imperceptibly.

"Nils, this is Brody, Valentina, Riley, Gabbie, and Leah," Alexsis says. She gives a hard look at the women. "Nils is here for *me*." The brunette, Valentina, gives her a feline grin in return as Brody fucks her. The others barely look up.

"Welcome," Brody says with his own grin. "Refreshments are at the back. Feel free to do — or don't do — whomever you want."

Alexsis leads me toward the back, where she quickly removes her blouse and chucks it onto one of the padded benches. Her skirt follows before I've so much as caught up to her. I do, however, note the bottles of water, condoms, and tray of little blue pills on offer. I smirk. Figures fuck-boy would need Mycoxafloppin.

I'm just glad there wasn't anything harder sitting out. That's not saying they don't do that shit, but at least it's not so much part of the repertoire that they don't bother hiding it. Even in my day, a joint here or there was fine. Maybe some ecstasy from time to time. But I wasn't into a lot of the crap the other models did. Coke. Meth. Heroine. You name it. All were a big no thanks from me.

I go to start undressing and freeze for a moment when I realize I'd thought the words "in my day." If young and taut Brody with his surfer boy blond curls and lean, muscled body didn't make me feel a little old, that sure as fuck did.

"You okay?" Alexsis asks, removing her bra.

I shake the thoughts off and whip my shirt over my head. "Never better," I assure her, prowling forward and capturing her lips with mine.

She sinks against me with a sigh, opening her mouth to me and sliding her tongue along mine in invitation. The sounds of skin-on-skin behind me remind me — and my cock — what we're doing here. My hands trace down the soft skin of Alexsis's sides, and I lift her leg, then drop down and plunge my tongue into her pussy.

Her fingers curl into my hair, scratching along my scalp as I lick and suck at her clit. She tugs lightly and I rise, picking her up as I go. Her legs wrap around me, and I turn us toward the side of the bed facing us. I lay Alexsis down on the empty strip of mattress behind Brody, Valentina, and the trio of blondes fucking each other before filling my mouth with her delicious pussy once more. As tempting as the toys on the wall are, right now I need to feel her, taste her.

But Alexsis clearly has other ideas as her fingers tug at my hair again. I tilt my gaze up to meet hers, continuing to suck at her clit, her lips, her juices while her eyes beg me for more.

"Fuck me," she whimpers.

One of the blondes screams in orgasm.

I pause and take a deep breath before the erotic soundtrack ripping through the room has me shooting off too soon.

I pull back, extracting the condom I'd brought from my back pocket. I unbutton and let my stiff cock spring forth then roll it on. I can barely stand the moans and groans ripping through the room. I yank Alexsis's legs toward me and give her everything she asked for and more, plunging in so deep and hard she cries out, joining the pleasure chorus, then leaning onto my arms to piston myself rapidly and roughly into her.

But only for a minute until I back off to slow and shallow. And then when she's begging for more, I go full bore again. Another woman's orgasm shatters through the base noise of moans and skin slapping together and my balls tighten. I back off again and look up to find Brody watching us with a smirk.

Alexsis's head tips back to follow my gaze, and I see the moment she locks eyes with Brody. She reaches one slender hand out toward his now-free cock, wrapping her long fingers around it. He groans and rips his eyes from her to look at me. His considerable ab muscles tense as he holds back, waiting for my permission.

I give it in the form of a raised eyebrow and small smile. Without hesitation, he scoots toward us, his lithe muscles rippling under his skin. I feel a churning behind my cock, so I slow down further until I'm lazily dipping in and out of Alexsis's tight cunt.

I watch as he leans over her, letting her take him into her mouth. As he fills her, fucks her, uses her hole. Alexsis's legs tighten around me, and I didn't need the impetus to unleash once more.

In a frenzy of thrusts, I hold her down with one hand while I rub her clit with the other. Our rhythms sync until both Brody and I are fucking her hard and fast from both ends. A feminine hand reaches between our bodies, tweaking Alexsis's nipples. I look up into Valentina's face. She licks her lips at me. I let out a disbelieving huff of a laugh and shake my head. With a small shrug, she focuses on Alexsis, dropping her mouth to suckle at her breast.

Alexsis pops her mouth off Brody's cock and gasps, clearly hanging on the edge of orgasm. "Oh fuck," she cries. "Harder, Nils, harder."

I oblige, even though bright light is starting to push at the edges of my vision, my own orgasm threateningly close. Alexsis's hand grips Brody's cock, pumping it as she continues to pant and moan. Brody's breathing picks up just as Alexsis's pussy tightens around me, and I realize all three of us are about to come.

The thought alone has my cock emptying as Alexsis screams her pleasure and Brody's cum spurts all over her chest. Valentina licks it up, and the sight sends Alexsis and me reeling, jerking into each other, release continuing to tear through us as my cries meet hers.

Once we're spent, the feeling starts to fade, and some semblance of self returns. I sway on the spot, overtaken by the post-orgasmic feeling of blissful emptiness. It's all I can do not to collapse on top of Alexsis.

Instead, I withdraw my hand from her clit with one last gentle swipe that causes her inner walls to flutter around my spent cock.

"Fuck," I groan.

Brody chuckles and, still hard thanks to the Viagra, lays on his back. The blonde who'd been eating out her friend suits him up and straddles him, using his stiff cock to get herself off while the others touch and lick her all over. Valentina starts to move away as well.

But not before saying to Alexsis and me, "I'd love to fuck you two sometime." She pinches Alexsis's nipple and winks at me before joining the others.

Surprisingly, Alexsis giggles, throwing her hands over her face before running them down her body. "That was ..." She sighs with happiness. It's a different kind of happy than I've seen on her before.

I lean down and kiss the spot at the crook of her

neck that she loves, driving my waning erection into her for a moment. She gasps and wriggles into me.

"That was unbelievable," I whisper into her ear. I press into her harder. "*You're* fucking unbelievable." Then I lean back and withdraw to deal with the condom.

When that's done, I grab a bottle of water and take a drink. Alexsis's hands slide around me from behind. I fold my hand over hers and turn toward her, offering her the rest of the bottle. She takes it, drinking deeply.

I run my hands lightly down her back. "So, what does round two look like?" I murmur.

She looks up at me contemplatively. "How about we go back to your place?"

I raise an eyebrow toward the bed where the sex toys have now been added to the mix and the women have paired up, kissing and biting and touching while riding double-ended dildos as Brody watches on.

"Unless you see something you like?" Alexsis asks sharply.

My eyes flick back to her, and I pull the water bottle from her hands, setting it back on the table. I pull her into my arms, my head dropping to lick her neck. "I'd be lying if I said I didn't want to fuck you as many ways as there are dildos in this room," I murmur against her skin. "But we can certainly do that at my place, too."

I pull back and Alexsis smirks up at me. "You have sex toys at your place?" she asks with a tone of disbelief.

I'm unable to fully suppress the wicked smile trying to break over my face. "Oh Alexsis, you have no idea," I reply, my tone laced with promise.

Her eyes go wide with excitement and her teeth sink into her lip. "On second thought, I may need one more orgasm before we leave," she admits.

I reach around her, wrapping my hand under her ass and feeling her pussy. My cock twitches between us at the wetness that coats my fingers. But he's not going to be of much use for a while yet, so I step back and gesture at the wall.

"Pick your pleasure, *Tessa*."

Her eyes glaze with lust and then flick to the wall.

"That one," she says, pointing to a triple-pronged pink dildo.

My eyebrows shoot up and my spent cock again jerks at the thought of all the screams and orgasms I'm going to pull out of her with that beast. And then I gladly get to work.

13

ALEXSIS

I'm utterly useless on Monday morning. Still boneless and mindless from orgasm after orgasm after orgasm. All the stress of yesterday's lunch gone.

Unfortunately, by the afternoon, the fact that I didn't tell Nils that he'd shortly be invited back to the Monaghan house sits heavy on my shoulders. I meant to last night. But taking Nils to the club … well, I thought it'd clear my mind enough to have that conversation. Turns out it distracted me completely. In a good way. But still, I know I need to talk to him about it soon.

Unfortunately, he calls me when I'm on my lunch break, well before I'm prepared to deal with it. Which would've been a welcome distraction but for the first words out of his mouth.

"Hey, beautiful. You'll never believe who I just heard from."

And suddenly I feel like I may lose my lunch. "Hey," I reply nervously. "Who'd you hear from?"

Please don't say Aiden, please don't say Aiden.

"Your brother, Aiden," he replies. *Well, fuck.* "Yeah, I'd emailed him after we ran into each other back in April but never heard back. Well, not until this morning anyway."

"Mmm, mmhm," I hum, waiting to see what Aiden actually said before I show my hand.

"He invited me to lunch with your family." And there it is. I should've prepared more for this, because I have no fucking clue what to say right now. After a minute of silence, Nils asks gently, "Is this what you were upset about last night?"

"No," I scoff indignantly. And then I crumple. I can't lie to Nils. Not now. Not about this. "Actually … yes. I'm sorry, I should've told you first. Aiden mentioned he'd found your email yesterday while I was having lunch at my family's house and my mom sort of suggested it."

Nils is quiet for a beat, and I try not to panic.

"And why did that upset you?" he finally asks in a reluctant tone.

I suck in a breath and my eyes dart around the

office. "Can we talk about this later?" I respond. "I'm kind of at work right now, remember?"

"Of course," he replies immediately. "I'm sorry. Stop by the club when you're off work? We can grab a bite at the diner."

"I mean … I might be here late. I'm doing a bunch of research for this new article I'm going after," I hedge. While it's true, I can't deny — to myself anyway — that this is a conversation I really don't want to have.

"Another night then," he replies quietly.

My chest aches at the disappointment in his voice. "No, I didn't mean that. I'll just … I'll do my best, okay?"

"Okay," he agrees. "Because the conversation about your family aside … I can't stop thinking about last night, Alexsis. I've been hard since I woke up."

My inner muscles clench and heat spreads through me. "Boy, you sure know how to motivate a girl," I murmur.

"I thought that might help," he replies with a chuckle. "I'll see you later?"

"With bells on."

. . .

"I'm shocked you chose food first," Nils teases as we take a seat in the familiar blue booths at the diner across from Baltia.

I narrow my eyes at him and pluck a menu from the holder against the wall. "Hey, food is important, too." I let out a sigh. "And I figured I might as well rip the band-aid off."

He raises an eyebrow and gestures for me to begin. Before I can, we're approached by a waitress, so I wait until we've ordered and she's out of earshot.

"You can't have lunch with my family," I blurt out.

Nils's brows pull together. "Why not?" he says simply, splaying his hands out on the table.

I chew at my lip and lean back into the booth, crossing my arms protectively over my chest.

"Do you remember anything about them at all?" I ask incredulously.

He tilts his head to the side, his eyes unfocused as he thinks about that. When they zero back in on mine, he leans forward. "I remember they were very nice people," he says carefully. "Much more authoritative than my own parents, but pleasant about it, nonetheless. Beyond that … well, I guess I mostly remember the time I spent with your brothers, Aiden in particular as we were the same age. Are the same age."

"You don't remember being dragged to church every Sunday?" I ask drily. Because lord if they didn't try their hardest to convert him.

"Vaguely?" he replies, his brow furrowing once more. "Why?"

I lean forward and rest my arms on the table. "They're Mormon, Nils. Like … old school LDS."

Nils raises an eyebrow. "I'm sorry, that doesn't mean anything to me," he replies, confused.

I let out an ironic laugh. "If you'd been anyone else, I'd be so fucking happy to hear you say that," I murmur, more to myself than him. Then distinctly to him, "You're so damn polite — and you're a man — so I can see how it didn't even register. But as a born and raised Mormon woman, as far as they're concerned anyway, well, their expectations of me are a little different."

"Different how?" he presses.

I scrunch my face and let out a sigh through my nose. "The short version is that there's no way in hell you can come to my family dinner. They simply can't know that we're dating," I reply, totally over-whelmed by the idea of explaining Mormonism to someone raised in one of the least religious countries in the world. And if I remember correctly, those in Sweden who are attend Lutheran churches; a *far* cry from LDS churches and all that entails, including the strict traditionalism, bizarre rules, and misogynistic attitudes, dress codes, and expectations.

"I'm going to need a little more than that," he prompts.

I let out another sigh. "My family — my father in particular — expect me to marry a Mormon man and pop out little Mormon babies for the rest of my life. The more the better. What they do *not* expect me to do is be with someone who is *not* Mormon, continue pursuing my own career, married or not, or — heaven forbid — not be totally sold on the idea of having kids at all."

Nils leans back with a contemplative expression. "I take it they don't know of your ah … previous career?"

I give him a wry smirk. "Definitely not."

"And your current job?"

I shift uncomfortably in my seat. "They know I write for a magazine," I hedge.

One of his eyebrows pops up. "But not what kind," he deduces.

"They know it's music?" I reply, heat creeping

into my cheeks. "But no, they don't know it's a rock magazine."

"Can they not find out themselves by googling you?" he points out.

I laugh. "Oh please, give me some credit. I write under Alex M."

"Ah," he says quietly. "Your friend Max Marshall's suggestion?"

"She inspired it," I admit. "But Max doesn't know a damn thing about my … upbringing. Or the other stuff."

The waitress appears with our food, and while she sets it out, even when responding to her, Nils's eyes are fixed on me in a way that makes me nervous.

I pick up a fry as soon as I get my plate to avoid making eye contact.

"So, your family doesn't know about your work or personal life … and those in your work and personal life don't know about your family," he accurately infers after the waitress is gone.

My eyes flick up guiltily to meet his. "You say 'personal life' like that goes beyond you," I joke.

"It doesn't?" he asks bluntly.

I lift a shoulder and pop another fry in my mouth. "I mean, Max and I are friends. But like … mostly coworker friends?" I let out a sigh. "I had a couple of other female friends in college, but one had a boyfriend who recognized me as Tessa, and that was that. Both of them refused to have anything to do with me after that." I blink hard against the sting of tears at being slut shamed for bitch number one's boyfriend trying to fuck me at a frat party. I shouldn't feel sorry for myself. I knew what doing porn could mean for my friendships. Not to mention putting up with the awful behavior of many of the men who'd recognize me in public.

"Well, I'm hardly one to criticize. Work has been my life as well. Though now Frankie and Julian are more like family than anything," he muses.

Something stirs in my chest as I suspect Nils might be a lot like me … lonely in some senses. I watch him in silence for a few minutes as he eats.

"Maybe I was too hasty," I finally say, realizing that being so hard lined on his coming for lunch could have serious implications for our relationship. A relationship that, surprisingly, I want. Badly. "Maybe you *could* come for lunch … if we leave this —" I gesture between us "— out of it."

Nils smirks and finishes the bite of burger he'd eaten, his throat bobbing. "You mean pretend we're not together."

I inhale deeply. "Yes," I admit.

He wipes off his hands and leans back, slinging an arm over the back of the booth, putting those arm muscles of his that I love on display. I lick my lips and look back at him.

"Can you really do that?" he asks earnestly, his gaze roving over my face.

I stare back at him, letting his ice-blue eyes devour me, feeling it all the way to my core. Can I really pretend I don't know what he looks like naked? The heat in his eyes while he watched me suck another man's cock? How much he makes me feel, despite myself?

"Yes," I reply confidently. If nothing else, being an adult film actress honed my faking-it skills. "I think the better question is, can you?"

Nils lets out a throaty laugh. "Considering I pretended not to be in love with my boss for *months*? Yes, I think I can manage one lunch."

My eyebrows jump in surprise. "Wait … you're in love with Frankie Greco?" My throat constricts at the thought, my stomach tumbling. There's no way in hell I can compete with Frankie Greco.

Nils's brow furrows and he leans forward, snatching my hand from the table and squeezing it reassuringly. "I *was* in love with her. I haven't been in quite some time," he assures me. I take a deep, steadying breath and nod. He strokes his thumb over the back of my hand. "So, your brothers don't even know?"

I snort. "The golden boys? That'd be a big no."

"They're both married and pumping out the kids, then?" he returns skeptically as if he already knows they're not.

I bark an ironic laugh. "Oh no. They're men. While they're expected to obey our parents the same as me … well, let's say our father asks quite a lot less of them. They'll be required to do both eventually, but I'm already practically an old maid in my dad's eyes." I don't add that it's probably only thanks to them both moving to L.A. that my father even considered letting me. Lord knows a woman can't live without a man watching her every move, making sure she doesn't do something to dishonor the family. Thank fuck neither of my brothers saw fit to actually follow through on Dad's directive to "keep an eye on" me.

Nils contemplates the information — and me — for a long moment. "What happens if they find out about us?"

My eyes go wide. "They can't, Nils. They'd disown me."

He frowns. "Is it wrong of me to say that I don't think that would be such a bad thing?"

I stare at him as I struggle to find my words. "Yes," I finally reply. "I mean, they're my parents."

Nils's frown deepens. "Your parents who not only don't accept and support you for who you are, but would actively shun you for it?" He shakes his head. "I'm afraid I don't understand. But then, I suppose ultimately, it's your decision."

I bristle at the judgment in his words. "Says the man who rarely goes back to his home country and family."

Nils pulls his hand away and gives me a sharp look. "I may not visit often, but I talk to my parents, my sister, regularly. It's because they support me that they don't expect me to leave the life I've built here — the life I love, that makes me happy."

I open my mouth to apologize, then close it out of embarrassment. Then open it again out of anger. "Forgive me if I can't shake a lifetime of programming that everything I want, everything I am, is considered shameful. If I can't just decide to live loud and proud at the expense of the only support system I've ever known," I snap, pulling back and wrapping my arms around myself.

"Well, that settles it," he says.

I give him a confused look. "Oh?"

His chin dips. "I'm going to lunch." I open my mouth, but he holds up a hand. "I promise I'll pretend like the last time I saw you was when we bumped into each other that first day. But I want to see what you see in them."

My whole body softens at his words. "If you're going for me … don't," I reply simply.

Nils shakes his head. "I'm sorry, Alexsis. But if these people are important to you, they're important to me, too. Hell, they *were* important to me once." He pauses. "I know that may not make sense to you, but I feel like I need to do this. Besides, I really would like to see Aiden again."

I take a shaky breath and decide against pointing out that he could see Aiden separately anytime. Because contrary to what he thinks, it does make sense. This is Nils wanting to be part of my support system in whatever way I'll let him.

While the thought terrifies and excites me in equal measure, I know this is one of those moments that's pivotal in a relationship. And if anyone is worth pushing through this terrifying ordeal for, it's Nils Larssen.

14

NILS

I've been sitting in front of Alexsis's parents' house for twenty minutes when an old van finally pulls into the driveway. I take a deep breath as it goes by before stepping out of the car and watching it disappear behind the garage door as it lowers.

I'm still unsure how I'm going to get through this. I'm torn between reuniting with the family I had such fond memories of and shoving down the less-than-charitable thoughts I have toward her parents at the possibility that they could truly disown their child for disobeying them. Their grown child. It seems simply too absurd, and I have to wonder if Alexsis might not be exaggerating because it's what she fears.

But the moment Aiden opens the door, my

125

concerns take a backseat as seventeen years collapse into nothing. Aiden's face breaks into the same genuine smile I remember, and I can't help grinning back.

"Nils! Man, it's really you." He pulls me into a warm embrace that feels both foreign and familiar. When we break apart, he's shaking his head in disbelief. "You look exactly the same. Well, except for the beard."

I run a hand over my jaw self-consciously. "It's good to see you, Aiden. You haven't changed much either."

That's mostly true. His blond hair is shorter now, more conservative, and there are faint lines around his eyes that weren't there before. But the warmth in his expression, the easy way he carries himself — the kind of calm, collected self-assurance that you can't help but be drawn to — that's all achingly familiar.

"Mom! Dad! Nils is here," he calls over his shoulder before stepping aside. "Come in, come in."

I follow him inside and a strong wave of nostalgia hits me. The house smells exactly as I remember — lemon cleaning products mixed with something sugary baking in the oven. Mrs. Monaghan — Izzy, as she always insisted I call her but could never bring myself to — appears from the kitchen, wiping her hands on an apron. Her face lights up when she sees me.

"Oh, Nils!" She pulls me into a hug that's surprisingly strong for such a small woman. "Look at you! So handsome. We've missed you so much."

She presses me back and I'm able to take in her graying hair and age-worn features. A reminder of how much time has truly passed since I last was here. And I can't help the warm feelings I have toward her, toward them all, despite what Alexsis has told me. Though I suspect the feeling won't last long if what she shared about them is true.

"It's wonderful to see you again, Mrs. Monaghan," I reply, the formality feeling strange on my tongue after years of casual American greetings. But I can't start calling her Izzy now. It would be too strange. Far too strange.

"Like I've always told you, Nils, call me Izzy. It's been a long time, but we still consider you practically family." She pats my cheek in a gesture so maternal it makes my chest tight.

Mr. Monaghan — Ammon, who has *definitely* never invited me to call him that — appears behind her, extending his hand for a firm shake. His grip is exactly as I remember: testing, measuring. "Good to see you again, son."

"You, too, sir," I respond stoically.

And then I see her. Alexsis emerges from the kitchen doorway, and it takes every ounce of self-control I possess not to react. She's wearing a modest blue dress that makes her grey-blue eyes brighter and covers her from neck to knee, her hair pulled back in a simple style. She looks nothing like the woman who rides me in silver dresses and demands I fuck her harder. She looks younger, somehow. And like a version of herself that's … constrained.

Our eyes meet for a fraction of a second before she drops her gaze.

"Come on," Aiden says, clapping me on the shoulder. "Let's catch up while the ladies finish lunch."

I follow him and Asher into the living room, hyperaware of Alexsis disappearing back into the kitchen with her mother. The men settle into well-worn deep-brown leather furniture that hasn't changed since I lived here, save some additional creases and aging that only adds to their comfortability. Some of the tension in my shoulders eases at the familiarity of it.

"So, you're managing nightclubs," Aiden says, leaning forward with interest. "That must be exciting."

"It has its moments," I reply carefully. "Though it's more paperwork than most people imagine."

Aiden chuckles. "Isn't that always the way? I spend more time in meetings about archiving than actually preserving anything."

We fall into easy conversation about our careers, and I'm grateful for the distraction. Ammon sits silent in his recliner, observing but not participating. His presence is a weight in the room, just as it always was. Though it has a different tenor now. Perhaps because I'm older. Or because I can't help feeling that he's what's holding Alexsis back from reconciling the two halves of herself. The fact that he has a book in his lap that I can just make out the title of — The Book of Mormon — is an ironic underscore to his severe countenance.

"Lunch is ready," Izzy calls, snapping me out of my thoughts.

We rise as one and migrate to the dining room. The table is set with the good china, that I know they only brought out to impress guests, and I find myself a bit flattered. Then my eyes lift to the side-by-side portraits behind the head of the table, behind Mr. Monaghan's usual chair. I remember them well, though their significance was lost on me then. But I did my research after everything Alexsis told me. And the symbolism of

Jesus and Joseph Smith flanking Ammon's seat, their austere gazes fixed on the family, isn't lost upon me.

Shaking off the somewhat creepy display of his power and authority as the head of the family, I take what I remember was my usual seat next to Aiden, directly across from Alexsis. I can't help recalling little Alexsis staring at me with big eyes across this very table all those years ago. Little did I know the already amorous thoughts she was having at such a tender age. I can't help the smirk that pulls at my lips. But this time, she keeps her eyes on her plate as we settle in. After Ammon says grace — another memory that hits unexpectedly hard, given what I know now — we begin eating in silence.

The pot roast is exactly as I remember, another familiarity that both soothes and chafes.

"This is delicious, Izzy. Just as good as I remembered," I offer.

She beams at the compliment. "Oh, you're too kind. I'm just so pleased you could join us. Tell us about your life, Nils. Aiden mentioned you manage nightclubs?"

"Yes, three of them, actually. All in Hollywood."

"My goodness. Hollywood. That sounds …" She frowns slightly while she clearly looks for a polite way to respond. "Well, that must keep you busy. What do you do when you're not working? Do you still attend church?"

I suppress a wry smile as the question lands exactly as she intended — pointed but polite.

"No, I don't," I respond succinctly.

"Oh." A pause as she likely considers her next attempt at staying on neutral topics. "Are you married? Any children?"

"Not yet … but maybe someday." I shrug nonchalantly to communicate how unimportant I find the conventions that seem to rule Americans' lives, then let my eyes slide over Alexsis as they move to Ammon on the other end of the table. Though he's diligently focused on his food, something tells me he's listening to every word.

Alas, I seem to have thwarted Mrs. Monaghan's attempts at pleasantries, and the silence that follows is suffocating. Alexsis shifts in her seat, and I catch the slight tightening around her eyes.

"Well," Izzy finally says, her tone forcefully bright, "it's just so wonderful to see you again. You know, we often talk about that year you stayed with us. You and Aiden were absolutely inseparable. He moped for months after you left."

"Mom," Aiden protests, pinkening around the ears. But he's smiling.

"It's true! Every day it was 'Nils this' and 'Nils that.'"

"We did keep in touch for a while," Aiden adds, shooting me a look that's almost apologetic. "But you know how it is. I got caught up with school, and then work ..."

"Life happens," I say, letting him off the hook. "I'm just glad we reconnected now. It's really good to see you." I look around. "All of you."

Another stretch of silence. The clink of silverware on china sounds unnaturally loud.

"So, Asher," Izzy says, her voice taking on a particular quality I can't quite place. "Have you and Katie set a date yet?"

Asher's jaw tightens almost imperceptibly. "Not yet."

"Well, don't wait too long. You're not getting any younger." She says it airily, but with an undertone of impatience that I don't miss.

Unfortunately, next she turns her attention to Alexsis, and I see my girl — because that's what she is, whether her parents know it or not — brace herself. I wonder if they notice.

"Alexsis, dear, I forgot to mention. David will be

meeting you here next Sunday after family time for your date. His eldest brother, Halden, will be chaperoning."

My brows pull together. "Chaperoning? I don't mean to intrude, but I'm not familiar with this word."

Izzy looks at me with surprise, as if she'd forgotten I wasn't part of their world anymore. "Oh! Well. It means … well, someone to go with them. It would be inappropriate for an unmarried woman to be alone with a man. Halden will accompany them to ensure Alexsis's reputation remains intact."

I set my fork down carefully, working to keep my voice neutral. "That's … an interesting custom." I try to say it diplomatically, but there's definitely a strain to my tone. "Is that usual even for adults?" My turn to ask pointed questions. And I give her a pointed look to match, in case it wasn't clear.

Apparently, it was, because the temperature in the room drops ten degrees. Ammon's voice cuts through the silence like a blade. "It absolutely is. No daughter of mine will be dishonored." He turns to Alexsis, and I watch her shrink under his gaze. "I expect you to start taking these suitors seriously, Alexsis. I want you married by next June."

The words hit me like a physical blow. "Why June specifically?" The words are out before I can stop them. I know as far as her parents are concerned that their daughter is none of my business. But I can't help it. I'm starting to see what she means, and my cool is slipping. Apparently along with my self control.

I expected Ammon to answer that it's none of my business, but it's Alexsis who offers, her voice barely above a whisper, "That's when I turn twenty-three."

As if that means something.

As if there's some … expiration date on unmarried Mormon women?

I don't know what.

But I must make some expression because Izzy's eyes narrow slightly as she watches me.

"Ah," I finally say, as if that settles everything.

Thankfully Asher jumps in to tell his father about a new marketing campaign he's spearheading and the rest of the meal passes in strained conversation.

When it's finally, mercifully over, I make my goodbyes as quickly as politeness allows. Ammon's handshake is perfunctory. Izzy's hug is a bit stiffer than before. Alexsis is nowhere to be found.

I kick myself internally for pushing like I did, hoping I didn't make things worse for her. For us.

Still, at least one good thing came out of it. I

forgot how much I liked Aiden. How well we get along. So I'll cling to that bright spot, at least.

"Call me," I tell Aiden as we embrace. "We should get dinner sometime. Catch up properly."

"I'd like that," he says, and I think he means it.

Asher gets a quick hug, too, and it's then that Alexsis re-emerges from the kitchen.

"It was nice to see you, Nils," she says sedately, as if she truly couldn't care less.

I step forward to give her a hug, because it only makes sense after hugging almost everyone else.

The air between us crackles with everything we can't say. I have to force myself to keep it brief and casual, but my arms linger around her a moment too long. Right now she smells like vanilla and cinnamon, not jasmine, and somehow that makes it worse. Like she's truly a different person.

"Good to see you, too," I manage.

And then I'm outside, gulping in air that doesn't taste of propriety and expectations. I make it to my car on autopilot, my mind spinning as I absorb how true everything Alexsis told me really is. What that means for her. For us.

15

ALEXSIS

I can't get out of my parents' house fast enough. Married by June. I knew my father would run out of patience. But it wasn't until he laid down the law — in front of Nils, no less — that I remembered he once said that a respectable Mormon woman is married before she's twenty-three. I remember asking him why, and his justification was that if her parents had permitted her to go to college, twenty-two was reasonable to still be unmarried. But after college? Well, there would be no reason to get a job, because a *respectable* Mormon woman would want to start having babies, of course.

The lack of logic and respect for personal choice shouldn't surprise me. And I guess I'm not. Humiliated is more like it. I warned Nils, but even I didn't expect either of my parents to behave that way in front of a guest. Though, I suppose Nils is different, since he was once part of our household, if only for a time.

I shake my head as I slip into my car and start the engine. And the next thing I do before I get the fuck out of here is text Nils.

Meet me at the club?

I'm not even to the freeway when I hear my phone ping. Once I hit the red light before turning on, I check his response.

On my way.

I breathe a sigh of relief, then crank the radio loud to drown out the maelstrom of thoughts in my head.

NILS IS ALREADY WAITING WHEN I PULL UP, LEANING against his car in the same designer jeans and black tee he'd worn to lunch, with the addition of a smoking hot leather jacket he hadn't been. I pull in next to him and step out.

"Hey," he says quietly.

I step up to him and look into his eyes. I can see

the pity there and it makes me even more disgusted with myself.

"You up for this?" I ask, hoping to dodge the conversation I sense coming.

He nods slowly. "But we need to talk first."

I can't help it; I roll my eyes and let out a long sigh. "Fine. You're probably right."

He reaches up and trails the back of his hand down my cheek.

"Are you really going on a date with this David?" he asks in a harsher tone than I'm used to hearing from him.

It makes my chest ache and pisses me off in equal measure. I shrug, wrapping my arms around myself. "I have to. It's part of keeping up the pretense of being the daughter they think I am."

"And what then? Are you going to marry him? Or someone like him? Keep up this charade forever?"

"Of course not," I snap. "Don't be silly."

"Then why?" He runs a hand through his hair, clearly frustrated. "You know this has to end, eventually. At the very least, you'll have to tell them you're not marrying a Mormon boy by next June."

"Don't ask me these questions." My voice cracks slightly. "I don't know, okay? You don't understand."

"You're right. I don't." He sounds so bitter and the ache in my chest expands. "I had a hard enough time pretending for one lunch. I can't imagine doing it for years, being someone I'm not."

I give him a sharp look. "Really? Because you did exactly that when you were in love with your boss and didn't tell her."

He staggers back as the intended blow lands. And though I meant the words to hurt, I instantly regret them.

"At least Frankie was just your boss," I continue, trying to soften the blow, to make him understand what I mean. How I feel. "It was just a job. These lies? They're to protect my relationship with the people who raised me, who love me, who support me."

"They may love you," he says quietly, "but they clearly don't support you. Not the real you."

Pain lances through me. It must show on my face as Nils holds his hands up in surrender.

"I'll let it go." He reaches out, touching my arm gently. "I know you came here to work off the stress from lunch. We should go inside."

Relief washes over me. The last thing I want to do is talk more about this. Think more about this.

"Thank you," I reply, placing my hands on his chest.

"What do you want to do in there?" he murmurs, stroking his thumb over the back of one hand.

I consider that for a moment. I breathe deeply. It has to be something special. Something that will make me forget everything else. That would make me feel like the center of *someone's* world, even if I'm not my parents.

"I want us to have a threesome with Brody," I say, then hold my breath as I tense for his rejection.

But to my surprise, he nods. "All right."

I bite into my bottom lip and go up on my toes to kiss him. I let all the anxiety and frustration out on his lips, writhing against him as I search for physical validation that our connection is still there.

He grips me to him and takes over, pressing my ass against my passenger door as his dick grows hard against my stomach. Finally, he breaks away, and we both pant as we lean our foreheads together.

"Come on," I say, tugging him gently toward the club.

He lets me lead him inside, to the purple room, where I can almost always count on Brody being.

And today is no exception, though it is exceptional that Brody is alone, wearing only a towel around his perfectly cut waist, wiping down surfaces and straightening pillows, either cleaning up from or preparing for a session. He looks up when we enter, his face breaking into a grin.

"Well, well, well. I was just about to head out, but I'm certainly glad I didn't." He tosses the cleaning cloth aside. "What can I do for my favorite couple tonight?"

With my fingers still twined in Nils's, I approach, getting right in Brody's space. I look up at him. "Up for a threesome?"

Brody's grin turns sly. "Oh, baby, you know I'm always up for *anything* that involves you." His eyes flick up to Nils. "I think the better question is, is lover boy?"

Nils's hand slides up my ass. "Anything to get this fucking dress off her."

I turn toward him, palming his semi-hard dick through his pants. "You don't like my dress?" I taunt.

Nils presses against me until my back is flush with Brody's front. "It's not you, love."

My breath catches at the endearment, and I tip my chin up. "Then take it off me," I breathe.

Nils obliges immediately, roughly yanking the

gingham print dress over my head and throwing it across the room, exposing my tits to the cold air.

"Fuck me," Nils groans, leaning in to capture a nipple in his mouth. I feel Brody's hands slide over my hips and I lean my head back against his shoulder.

"Oh, you will," I promise, tilting my head. "But … would you fuck *him* first?" I slide my hand over Brody's very hard cock, yanking the towel until I feel the silken length against my backside. I slide my hand gently up and down as I watch Nils contemplate my request.

After a few beats, Brody chuckles behind me. "I don't think lover boy and I are … compatible," he murmurs in my ear loud enough for Nils to hear, too. Nils smirks as if in agreement.

My face scrunches in confusion. "How's that?"

Brody's hand slides to my sex, gently stroking as Nils rejoins, tugging at my nipples. "See, I know I'm a top. And I'm pretty sure he is, too."

I roll my eyes. Men. Always wanting to dominate. I pull Nils toward me, switching to stroking his cock now. "Is that true?" I ask, batting my eyelashes at him.

"It's true," he confirms. "But I'm more than happy to do whatever you want to this body." He slides his hand between us, thrusting his fingers abruptly into the heat between my legs.

I arch, sighing out my pleasure. "Fill all my holes," I say on a sigh. "Please, daddies."

And so, they do. Both totally focused on me, working in tandem. One fucking my mouth while the other fucks my pussy, then switching. It's everything … and yet somehow not enough. That is, until I'm riding Nils's cock and Brody decides to move from my mouth to behind me.

I've done double penetration, but it's not part of our usual repertoire, given that both Brody and I prefer a harem of women around us. But as he lightly runs the tip of his lubricated-condom-covered cock over my ass, waiting for permission, I realize it's exactly what I need. I did say "fill all my holes" after all.

"Yes, daddy," I groan. "Fuck my ass while he fucks my cunt."

Nils grows harder inside of me. I look down at him with a feline grin. "You like the dirty talk?" He nods. "You want him to fuck me while you do?" Nils lets out a strangled groan of agreement, so I swirl my hips over him before stilling for Brody. His hot, hard cock pushes in slowly, and a feeling of complete fullness and mind-numbing bliss washes over me. "God, yes, give me that cock. Fill me up," I encourage him. He keeps pushing until he's in to the hilt.

Sandwiched between them, I don't have to tell either what to do. They both start moving in turn, one in while the other pulls out, thrusting and fucking in a way no dildo could ever replicate.

And the pleasure … it's heaven.

A filthy diatribe of barely controlled thoughts spills from my mouth, encouraging them to take me, to fuck me, to use my holes, that I'm their little slut, that I want them to fuck me until they come. Then as the intensity builds, to spill all over my ass, in my cunt.

They get sweatier and harder and faster until I can't hold back the rising tide of pleasure and I come hard, speechless, mindless, lost to this, finally. Nils comes with me, his thrusts stuttering while Brody's stay true.

It's only when he stills that Brody pulls out, rips off his condom, and comes all over my ass. The hot, sticky cum drips down my side beautifully, and Brody collapses on top of us.

My mouth meets Nils' as Brody sucks at my neck.

"You're a fucking goddess, Tessa," Brody groans.

"My goddess," Nils whispers against my skin.

I grin, languishing in their attentions. Brody rolls off onto the bed next to us.

I wiggle over Nils, his flagging cock slipping out with a gush of his cum.

"That was …" I trail off, shivering.

Nils cocks an eyebrow. "Then you'll love what comes next." My eyebrows pop up as Nils lifts me as he sits up, setting me between Brody's legs. Brody scoots up onto his elbows with a questioning look at Nils. "Hold her up and fuck her ass while I eat her pussy?"

My whole body tightens at his words. "Yes, god, please, yes," I beg, whimpering.

Brody grins, suiting up and letting Nils lift me over Brody's supine form. I brace my hands as Brody's settle under my thighs, as his cock slowly settles back into my ass. He pumps slow and deep and spreads me open for Nils.

I look down as he positions himself between my legs. "You gonna lick all my juices and your cum off me?" I taunt him.

"You want that?" he murmurs, tracing a finger down my slit, causing me to spasm under their ministrations.

"Yes. Now, please," I beg.

Nils chuckles but then wastes no time. He uses

only his tongue at first, licking me clean until I'm dripping wet again anyway, then adding fingers into the mix. Brody picks up his pace as Nils works, until I'm boneless and overwhelmed … and coming so hard I see stars.

Brody slides me down his body onto the bed where I lay, star-fish style, with a huge grin on my face.

Nils slides in next to me, tilting my head his way to place a claiming kiss on my lips. I curl into him, and Brody spoons me from behind.

"That was perfect," I murmur against Nils's chest. "Thank you, daddies."

Brody kisses my shoulder as Nils strokes my hair. I'm so relaxed I start to drift off.

I don't fall asleep, exactly, hovering somewhere between conscious and unconscious on a sea of sparkling bliss and contentment.

But they must *think* I'm asleep, because I'm fully aware when Nils asks Brody, "How often are you here?"

"Every day," Brody replies, his fingers brushing my hip possessively. "But I always look forward to the days Tessa drops by."

"Well, that's a shame she won't be coming by as often, then." Nils's tone is hard.

Brody laughs, the sound knowing. "We'll see."

"What's that supposed to mean?"

And I can almost hear the pity in Brody's voice when he responds, "I'm not worried about losing her, man. None of her boy toys stick around long. She always comes back to me. So, even if she's not around as much right now, she'll be back."

The challenge in his tone stirs me enough to bring me back to the moment. "Now, now, daddies," I grumble, stretching like a cat and running my claws down their chests. "We were having such a wonderful moment. Don't ruin it."

Brody slides out of bed, and one look at his face tells me he's more irked by Nils than I realized. "Nothing ruined," he says, his voice overly casual. "I have to go, anyway. Nice playing with you, Tessa. See you soon." And with that he grabs his towel, leaving without even wrapping it around his waist.

"Well," I say to Nils. "I know you didn't like him much, but clearly the feeling is mutual."

Nils grunts his agreement. "Clearly."

I run my nails over his nipple. "Funny, because you two fuck me so well together."

Nils's cock twitches between us and he leans in, kissing me long and sweetly. "That's all you. You're the magic here. Not that dickhead."

I laugh, scraping my nails over his stomach now. "He's not so bad. You're just both territorial."

Nils huffs. "He's in love with you, you know."

I snort. "Dogs fight over bitches in heat. That doesn't mean they love them." Nils gives me a skeptical look. I shake my head. "You don't know him like I do. He's definitely not in love with me."

Nils doesn't respond immediately. But eventually asks, "Are you sure about that?"

"Yes, I'm sure. Brody doesn't do feelings. Trust me." I sit up, over this conversation. It's letting the doubt and worry that is my life creep back in. "Let's not let that little pissing match ruin our night, okay?"

Nils sits up beside me, pulling me between his legs. "I'm here if you want to talk. About any of it, you know."

And I do know. I also know he doesn't mean Brody. He means my parents. And that I decidedly do *not* want to talk about. In fact, the less talking we do tonight, the better.

"I know. And I appreciate it. But what I really need right now is to go back to your place and test out some of these toys you say you have," I respond coyly, climbing fully into his lap, letting my breasts brush his chest.

His hands slide up my back and he sighs. "Go put

that god awful dress back on. But only so I can take it off again as soon as possible."

I tip my head back and laugh. And I secretly love that he hates that disguise. That he doesn't want anything but the real me.

"Deal," I agree.

16

ALEXSIS

I t's with some very mixed feelings that I start the workweek. All the confusion of my father's latest demand-slash-deadline on top of everything getting deeper and more complicated with Nils and … well, I'm pretty damn happy to have work to distract me. Especially today. Because after weeks of preparation for the article idea that's been consuming me, things are getting real.

I did as much research as I could, then made a call, and now, after making a token appearance at the office, I've snuck out to take it to the next level. Which is why, at ten on the dot, I'm pulling up to a modest house in the Valley where James Kennedy, Violent Mood Swings' keyboardist, has his home studio.

This is it. This is the story that's going to change everything. You wouldn't expect that the small, ramshackle rancher houses one of our times' most famous musicians, but here we are. Walking up to the house, broken pavers litter the path, and toys are scattered all over the lawn.

I knock, my tummy a bundle of nerves. But when James opens the door, he's exactly what you'd expect from a dad-rocker with his kind eyes, slightly rumpled short-sleeved polo and flannel over well-worn jeans, and easy smile that probably still makes groupies swoon. It definitely puts me more at ease, anyway.

"Alexsis, right?"

I nod and smile. "That's right. I'm surprised you remember me."

"Really?" he asks with a laugh. "You were all over that apology tour."

I blush hard. "Yeah, but most guys in your position wouldn't notice one of the peons sent to follow them around," I reply honestly.

He steps back in invitation, so I cross the threshold. "Well, most musicians are assholes, I'll give you that." He laughs. "Anyway, come on in. The rest of the band is already here."

I follow him through a house that screams "family" – even more toys than outside scattered in corners, crayon drawings on the fridge, the faint smell of baby powder mixing with coffee. It's such a contrast to the rock star image that I have to hide my smile. He really isn't your typical famous musician.

When we finally get to his studio, the large space — which I think is a converted garage — is packed with instruments, a couch, and a few mismatched chairs. And, of course, the rest of the band.

West nods at me from where he's sitting backwards on a folding chair, his dark hair and leather jacket still screaming his bad boy image, even though I know he's left that behind. Ward is sprawled on a worn leather couch, all lanky arms and legs and shaggy blond hair, tattoos snaking down both lean, muscled arms. The newer members are the only ones behind their instruments —Michael being on the drum kit tapping out a quiet rhythm, and Nik cross-legged on the floor, bass in her lap. They all somehow look comfortable and pissed off at the same time. Rock stars.

"Thanks for agreeing to talk to me," I start, pulling out my recorder and notebook. I take a subtle deep breath to calm my nerves. It's not like I haven't done this before. Though that was almost always with — or for — Max. This is all me. No pressure.

"Are you kidding?" Ward says, leaning forward. "Someone actually wants to hear our side. We've been waiting for this." Everyone nods in agreement, and my nerves mellow a bit more. Enough to start down the list of questions I prepared, anyway.

Some of the answers are exactly what I expected. But many aren't and frankly make my blood boil. They tell me about signing their first contract when they were barely legal adults. How the label's lawyers sat them down and "explained" everything, assuring them they didn't need their own representation.

"They said it was standard," West says bitterly. "Said they were looking out for us."

"Standard my ass," Michael adds. "They own everything. Every song Violent Mood Swings has ever written under that contract. Every version of the band name. Hell, they probably own the air we breathed in their studios." Nik snorts.

Then Ward jumps in, explaining how they'd tried to release new music independently after getting back together, only to be hit with cease and desist letters, both facts I knew. "It just … it sucks. How can we not even use our own fucking name? I mean, we came up with it in my garage when we were teenagers."

"It's legalized theft at best," James says quietly. "But honestly? If it was just us … well, I guess we could figure out how to move on. But the worst part is, this is happening to bands everywhere. It's not a one-off. It's how the industry operates. Taking advantage of young kids who just want to make music by getting them locked into contracts that basically make them indentured servants." He shakes his head, and every member of the band makes their own noise of agreement.

They all have tidbits and examples to add, and by the time I leave, my notebook is full and my recorder has enough material for a whole *series* of articles. And I have so many ideas of who I could interview next to flesh this out.

I hadn't realized what pulling at this thread would unravel. Because this is huge. This could expose the whole industry's corrupt practices and help change how young musicians approach recording contracts. Or hell, whether they even go that route. Other options are opening up these days, after all.

The thought of being part of such a huge shift … well, I'm practically vibrating with excitement as I walk back into the *Rock Scene* office after lunch. I need to transcribe these interviews immediately, start organizing the story structure, schedule more interviews —

"Alexsis. My office. Now." Jason's voice cuts through my plans like a bucket of ice water. I follow him, noting the tense set of his shoulders. "Where were you this morning?" he asks as soon as the door closes.

I try to deflect by keeping it vague, knowing it won't fly. "Working on a story."

"What story?"

"Just ... following up on some leads." Shit. Shit, shit, shit, shit. Pulling this off hinged on his not noticing. I should've been more careful. Come up with a better story if he did notice. As good as I am at lying to my parents, right now I can't think of a good enough story to give Jason that he'd actually buy.

His eyes narrow, as if he smells blood in the water. "Alexsis, I'm not going to ask again. And if you don't answer, we're going to have a disciplinary discussion about transparency and following proper channels."

Shit. I sink into the chair across from his desk. There's nothing to go with but the truth at this point. "I was interviewing Violent Mood Swings about their legal troubles with their former label."

The color drains from Jason's face. "You did what?"

"It's a great story, Jason. They're being completely screwed over —"

"Absolutely not." He's on his feet now, pacing behind his desk. "Do you have any idea what kind of legal shitstorm you could bring down on us? That label has deeper pockets than God. They could bury us in lawsuits just for fun. If they even got wind you talked to the band about the lawsuit, we could be in a world of hurt, Alexsis."

"But it's the truth! People deserve to know —"

"Not from us they don't." His tone brooks no argument. "You're not writing this. You're not pursuing this story. In fact, you're going to delete whatever notes and recordings you have."

I stand, too, anger flooding through me. "You can't be serious."

"Dead serious. This is non-negotiable, Alexsis. You have no idea what kind of power they have. We're a small magazine. We'd be a tiny bug on the windshield of their Bentleys, I promise you. Do you want us all to lose our jobs?" He shakes his head in disgust. "Get out of my sight." He waves me off angrily, sitting back down so hard his chair creaks in protest.

I storm out of his office, my hands shaking with rage. All that work. All that potential to actually make a difference. Gone because Jason is too scared of the big bad record label. What about the fact that it'd be a bad look to instantly crush a magazine that criticized you? Wouldn't that prove to everyone that we were right? I need to vent about this. Badly.

Thankfully, I find Max in her cubicle and collapse into her spare chair.

"Let me guess," she says after one look at my face. "Jason killed your story."

"How did you —"

"Because I warned you this might happen." Her tone is gentle, not gloating. "The magazine can't afford to take on that kind of fight. And even if we did anyway, it wouldn't change anything."

I look up at her. "What do you mean?" I ask.

Max sighs and leans forward. "Once you've been around a while, you start seeing the corruption. You get angry, at first. You want to expose it. But then you realize you can't expose something when the people you're after own the press, Alexsis. There is no world in which we win, in any way."

I shake my head, not wanting to believe her. But … the evidence is on my tape recorder. Well, until I'm forced to delete it, anyway.

"It's not fair," I mutter, knowing I sound like a petulant child but not caring.

"No, it's not." Max turns to face me fully. "But you know what? You're smart enough to find another angle. Another story. Something even better. Something that you can bring to the public's attention that *can* make a difference in the industry."

"You really think so?"

"I know so. You're a talented writer and you have that fighting spirit, Alexsis. One setback isn't going to stop you."

Her faith in me is touching, even if it doesn't quite ease the sting of disappointment. I thank her and head out, needing air, needing space, needing ...

Nils.

I don't know why he's the person I want to see, but twenty minutes after I'm done at work, I'm walking into Baltia. It's early evening, so the club is just starting to come alive. I find him in his office, door open, bent over some paperwork.

"Hey," I say, knocking on the doorframe.

He looks up, and something warm flickers in those ice-blue eyes. "Alexsis. This is a pleasant surprise."

"Bad day," I admit, sinking into the chair across from him. "I thought maybe..."

I trail off as a rhythmic thumping starts from somewhere around us, accompanied by unmistakable moans. My eyes widen as I realize what we're hearing.

Nils sighs. "They must be in a good mood because usually it's only Sunday afternoons."

"Frankie and Julian?"

He nods, looking mildly exasperated. "I've learned to schedule my office time accordingly, but sometimes they can't resist."

An idea strikes me, bold and totally inappropriate, but my frustration needs an outlet. "We could make it a foursome."

Nils's head snaps back to me. "What?"

"You know, join them. Could be fun. Girls only touch girls, of course."

"Are you serious? No." His response comes out so sharply I blanch.

"Why not?" I challenge. "Still carrying a torch for the boss?"

He scoffs. "That's not — Alexsis, if I asked you to have a foursome with a couple where one of them was someone you used to be in love with — or was your boss ... or fuck, *both* — how would you feel?"

"I'd be fine with it," I say stubbornly. "It's just

sex. Funny how you can't separate sex and feelings, yet I can."

"I can separate them just fine most of the time," he says, his jaw tight.

"Good. Then maybe we could organize an orgy at the club instead."

"Would that include Brody?"

The question catches me off guard, even though it shouldn't. "Probably, why?"

"I'd rather he not be at every encounter we have."

Anger flares in my chest, mixing with all the frustration from earlier. "Are you seriously trying to tell me who I can and cannot fuck? Because that's not how this works, Nils."

I'm on my feet and heading for the door before he can respond, my emotions a tangled mess of professional disappointment and personal fury.

It's not until I'm home, after a long shower and half a bottle of wine, that I realize what I've done. I took all my anger about the article, about Jason shutting me down, about my career feeling stalled, and I dumped it on Nils.

He wasn't trying to control me. He was trying to

tell me he wanted some encounters that didn't include Brody. And I threw it in his face because I was upset about something that had nothing to do with him. God, I suggested we waltz in on his boss, who he'd once been in love with, and ask if we can join them. What the hell is wrong with me? A lot, is the answer.

"Fuck," I mutter to my empty apartment.

I owe him an apology. And maybe more than that, I owe him some honesty about where I'm at. Why I really pushed too far, too hard today. And what I really want from whatever this thing between us is becoming. Because the truth is, the thought of him with Frankie made me feel something I wasn't prepared for either, adding to the fuel of the dumpster fire that is my life right now. Not that it's an excuse for how I behaved tonight.

But that's tomorrow's problem. Right now, I'm going to wallow in my professional disappointment and try not to think about the hurt that flashed in Nils's eyes before I stormed out. It'll all get fixed. I hope.

Though why I bother hoping for anything these days is beyond me.

I sink my head back into the couch. It's official:

I've fully devolved into a pity party. Get a grip on your life, Alexsis, before you ruin everything that's good about it.

It's the last thought I have before, drunker than I thought, I pass out.

17

NILS

I stare at the clock on my kitchen wall. Two in the afternoon. Normally, I'd be heading to Baltia right about now to catch up on paperwork, check the inventory, review the upcoming bookings. But today, the thought of going to my office — where just yesterday Alexsis suggested we interrupt Frankie and Julian's afternoon activities — makes my stomach turn.

Instead, I pour myself another cup of coffee and sink onto my couch. The silence of my apartment presses in on me, but it's better than the alternative. Better than running into Emma, who's still shooting me daggers every chance she gets. Better than potentially seeing Alexsis if she decides to show up again.

I'm overwhelmed. That's the word for this

crushing weight on my chest. Alexsis is clearly spin-ning out of control, and I don't know how to help her. Hell, I don't even know if she wants my help. The way she stormed out yesterday ...

And underneath it all, there's this constant simmer of anger I have toward her parents and the impossible position they've put her in. The way they're forcing her to live this double life that's clearly tearing her apart.

Before I can think better of it, I pick up my phone and place a call. It's not too terribly late in Sweden, and I know they'd answer even if it were.

"Hej, son." My father's warm voice fills my ear, and immediately some of the tension leaves my shoulders.

"Hej, Pappa." I switch to Swedish without thinking, the familiar sounds of home wrapping around me like a blanket. "How are you and Mamma?"

"We're well. But you don't sound it. What's wrong?"

I lean back, closing my eyes. Trust my father to cut straight to the heart of things. "I'm ... dealing with a complicated situation."

"A woman?"

I huff a laugh. "How did you know?"

"Because you're my son, and I know that tone. Tell me about her."

So I do. Not everything — I leave out the more intimate details — but I tell him about Alexsis, about her family situation, about the pressure she's under. About how she's lashing out and I don't know how to help.

My father is quiet for a long moment after I finish. "This woman, she's important to you?"

"Yes," I admit to him and myself at the same time. "Very."

"Then be patient. She's carrying a heavy burden, trying to be two different people. That would break anyone. Give her time to figure out who she really wants to be."

"But what if she never figures it out? What if she just keeps doing things that push me away?"

"Then at least you'll know you tried. But Nils, from what you've told me, she sounds strong. She just needs someone to be steady while she finds her balance."

I absorb that for a moment. "When did you get so wise?"

He chuckles. "When you moved halfway around the world and I had to learn to give advice over the phone. Your mother wants to talk to you."

There's rustling, then my mother's voice. "Nils, darling. I was listening — well, to your father's end of the conversation, anyway."

"Of course you were," I say with a smile. "And what's your advice, Mamma?"

"My advice is to take your father's advice … but also, don't sit at home brooding. Go see friends. Distract yourself. It won't help her or you if you're sitting around overthinking everything."

I sigh heavily. "You're right. Thank you. I love you, Mamma."

"We love you, too. And Nils? Thank you for calling. Not all children would think to reach out to their parents when they're struggling."

The words hit differently after everything with Alexsis's family. "You and Pappa have always been there for me. Even when I moved here. Even when I chose a completely different life than you'd imagined for me. I'm grateful for that."

"Oh, darling." Her voice is thick with emotion. "We just want you to be happy."

"I miss you. All of you. Tell Astrid I love her, too."

"We miss you, too, and so does your sister. I'll tell her. Take care, hjärtat."

"Bye, Mamma."

I laugh, shaking my head once I've hung up. Only my mother can get away with calling me "sweetheart." But it's why I called them — they know me better than anyone. I'd be a fool not to listen to them.

I think about what they both said, my mother's advice in particular echoing in my head. Don't sit around brooding. Go see friends.

I scroll through my phone and stop at Aiden's number. We'd exchanged information after the lunch at his parents' house, but neither of us had reached out yet. Even though I invited him to, he's already done so once. Maybe now it's my turn.

He answers on the second ring. "Nils? Hey, man. I was actually going to call you this week."

"Yeah? What about?"

"That dinner we talked about. You free tonight?"

I glance around my empty apartment. "Actually, yes. That sounds perfect."

"Great. How about Musso & Frank's? Say, seven?"

"Sure, yeah, I love that place. See you there."

The rest of the afternoon passes more quickly with plans to look forward to. I shower, change into dark jeans and a burgundy button-down, and arrive at the historic Hollywood restaurant right on time.

Aiden's already there, seated in one of the iconic red leather booths. He stands when he sees me, and we embrace briefly before sitting across from each other.

"You sounded a little off on the phone," Aiden says after we've ordered drinks. "Everything okay?"

I fidget with my water glass. I can't tell him about Alexsis — not when I don't even know if she'd want her brother to know we're ... whatever we are. "Just work stress. Managing a nightclub isn't always glamorous."

"I bet." He leans back, studying me. "You know, it's still surreal seeing you after all these years. I never imagined when you left our house that you'd end up staying this long."

"Life has a way of surprising us."

"That it does." He pauses as our drinks arrive — scotch for him, a martini for me. "Speaking of surprises ... I'm seeing someone."

I raise an eyebrow, noting the careful way he says it. "That's great."

"His name is Josh." The words come out in a rush, like he's been holding them in too long. "We've been together for two years."

I smile. "He makes you happy?"

The relief on Aiden's face is palpable. "Yeah. He

really does. My parents ... they don't know, obviously."

"Obviously," I echo, thinking of all the things Alexsis can't tell them either.

"God, it feels so good to tell someone." He smiles, clearly genuinely happy. "Actually, that reminds me." Aiden leans forward, lowering his voice. "You haven't told Alexsis our secret, have you?"

I freeze with my martini glass halfway to my mouth. "What? No. Why would you think I'd even be in a position where that would come up?"

"I don't know, just ... I know Alexsis said you guys just ran into each other at that concert the one time ... but at lunch, it seemed like there was something there. Chemistry. I thought maybe it was more than just that one meeting?"

He eyes me speculatively. And my discomfort must show on my face because Aiden's eyes widen slightly.

"I'm right, aren't I? You two are seeing each other."

I set down my martini carefully. "I'm not sure what to say to that."

A knowing smile spreads across his face. "You are. Holy shit. You're dating my sister."

"Aiden —"

"No, it's okay. I mean, it's weird, but it's okay." He pauses. "Look, I suspected you guys might be together and I just ... I didn't want ancient history to complicate things between you two if you were."

I grimace, thinking about how Alexsis has never told her brothers about her time as Tessa Temptation. How she'd probably be fine with the fact that her brother and I had brief but memorable encounters all those years ago. But I can't tell Aiden about her secrets any more than I can tell her about ours.

"It won't," I say finally. "We agreed to keep it between us back then. That hasn't changed."

"Good. Good." He takes a long drink. "God, the secrets we all keep from our parents. From each other. Sometimes I wonder if it's worth it."

"Yeah," I agree quietly, feeling the weight of all these lies and half-truths. "Me, too."

We manage to steer the conversation to safer topics after that — his work, my adjustment to American life becoming permanent, memories from when I lived with his family. But underneath it all, I can't shake the feeling that we're all trapped in an elaborate web of secrets that's going to collapse eventually.

It's late when I finally get home, and I'm getting

ready for bed when my phone buzzes. Alexsis's name lights up the screen.

"Hey," I answer, confused and relieved to hear from her in equal measure.

"Hey. Can we talk?" Her voice is small, uncertain.

"Of course," I assure her.

"I'm sorry about yesterday. I was completely out of line."

I sink onto my bed. "I … appreciate you saying that. Because honestly you were. But that was out of character, even for you, Alexsis. What was that really about?"

Alexsis sighs heavily and starts back at that morning, about the article I know she'd been pursuing, sharing that she'd interviewed the band and was on cloud nine only to go back to work and get shut down hard by Jason. About how all that frustration and disappointment got channeled into jealousy when she heard Frankie and Julian, and knew it was something I regularly heard happening.

"I was already feeling like everything was out of control," she says. "And then hearing her, knowing you'd been in love with her, wondering if it brought up those feelings again ... I just lost it. It made me so fucking jealous. It was irrational and unfair, I know, and I'm so sorry."

"Alexsis." I keep my voice gentle. "I understand. You're under a lot of pressure."

"That's not an excuse for how I behaved."

"No, but it's an explanation. And I appreciate you telling me."

"Can you forgive me?"

"I already had. I know what you've been going through Alexsis. I mean … I may not *know* know, since I'm not in your position. But I get that this is all a lot. Fuck. I'm not saying this right at all. This is just … doing this over the phone … it's not enough. Can you come over?"

There's a pause. "Now?"

"Now."

"I'll be there in twenty minutes." I can hear the smile in her voice, and my own lips spread in a grin.

"Hurry," I urge her. A click is my only response.

I'm not waiting long — only fifteen minutes — before there's a knock on the door. When I open it, she looks smaller somehow, vulnerable in a way she rarely allows herself to be. I pull her into my arms without a word and close the door behind her.

"I'm sorry," she whispers against my chest.

"I know." I tilt her chin up. "We're okay."

When I kiss her, it's soft, careful. An acknowledgment of the fragility between us right now. She melts into me, running her hands over my chest.

I pull back and caress her face, slipping my hand gently around hers and leading her to my bedroom.

I undress her slowly, then myself. She lays down on the black sheets, sliding to the head of the bed, opening her legs invitingly. Still with that look of vulnerability about her.

I prowl slowly up the bed, placing a kiss at her ankle. Then her calf. Then her knee, then the inside of her thigh.

Her fingers slide into my hair as my tongue meets her sex, and she lets out a breathy sigh. I part her with two fingers and lick slowly, thoroughly until she's writhing under me. And then I rear up, gripping my hard length, stroking up and down. She licks her lips and whimpers. A small smile tugs at the corner of my mouth.

And then I enter her. Slowly. Sweetly. Until I'm as deep inside of her as I can be. Until her warmth wraps around me. Then I wrap myself around her and move. It's intense and quiet and simple. Sex like we've never had before.

No games, no power plays, just two people trying to find their way back to each other.

Her hands skim down my back, and my lips find hers again while I continue to piston my hips. She shudders against me, her walls fluttering around my cock.

"Yes," I whisper to her. "Come for me, Alexsis. Only me."

She nods, her chin tipping up as she tightens around me. The velvet grip she has on my cock pushes me into orgasm and I come so hard I sink into her neck, groaning my release.

Her hands find my face, pulling my lips to hers. She kisses me with a depth she never has before. It's apology and penance and a promise all at once.

And I know in this moment that I'll be whatever she needs for as long as she needs. So long as I get to be here, with her.

I pull away, running my nose down hers. "Be right back."

I go to the bathroom and do a quick clean-up, bringing back a warm, wet rag for Alexsis. She smiles when she sees me with it, spreading her legs, baring her sex to me. I sigh, settling down next to her and running a finger through her wet warmth, the evidence of our pleasure coating my fingertips. She wiggles against my hand, and I fight the urge to keep going. I want to hold her more right now. So I clean her up gently, though I'm unable to resist swirling the cloth over her clitoris a bit harder than necessary. She bites her lip and giggles when I do. With a smile, I toss the cloth into the laundry bin in the corner and settle next to her.

She curls against my side, tracing patterns on my chest.

"I'd love to spend all night making up, but I really should get home so I can get some actual sleep," she laments.

I huff out a dry laugh. "Don't worry, we can make up again another night," I tease.

"Sunday?" she asks hopefully.

"After church?"

She tenses slightly. "Actually ... I was thinking maybe we could skip the family lunch. Just spend the day together."

I press a kiss to her forehead. "Whatever you need."

"What I need," she says quietly, "is to figure out how to be myself. All the time. Not just when I'm with you."

"You'll get there," I promise, vowing silently to do whatever I can to make that happen. Even knowing it's really up to her.

I pull her against me. One last feel of her skin

against mine. One last reminder of how well we fit together. Like she was the piece of me I'd been missing. Like maybe I'm one of the pieces *she's* been missing. Though I know there are more. Ones she needs to find for herself.

But for now, she's here in my arms, and that's enough. Right now, nothing else matters.

18

ALEXSIS

The next morning, I knock on Jason's office door with a determination I haven't felt in days. I may not be able to fix all of my problems, but I can fix this one.

When he calls me in, I sit on the edge of the chair opposite his desk, allowing my anxiety and chagrin to be on full display. An offering of my regret.

"I owe you an apology," I start before he can say anything.

His eyebrows rise, but he leans back in his chair, giving me space to continue.

"I pursued that story because I saw an opportunity. I wanted to be worthy of my own byline, and I thought this could be it. But I didn't look at the bigger picture for the magazine. I didn't consider the fallout." I take a breath. "I promise to come to you before pursuing something like that in the future. Though I'd also like you to be more willing to let me prove myself."

Jason is quiet for a long moment, studying me. "Thank you for the apology, Alexsis. I appreciate it. And you're right — I should give you more opportunities. I was only so angry because ..." He pauses, seeming to choose his words carefully. "Because I think highly of you. Your talent. Your potential. I was disappointed by the lack of consideration, not the ambition."

The compliment catches me off guard, and I feel heat rise to my cheeks. "Thank you. That means a lot."

"Good. Now get back to work and find me a story that won't get us sued into oblivion."

I smile and nod, leaving his office with renewed energy.

He thinks highly of me. My talent. My potential.

And I'm going to find a story that proves him right.

The rest of the week flies by in a blur of productivity. I bounce idea after idea off Max, who praises each one enthusiastically.

"This one about the underground music scene in Koreatown? Brilliant," she says Wednesday.

"The profile on female drummers breaking barriers? Love it," she adds Thursday.

By Friday, when I suggest a piece on how streaming services are changing the way artists approach album creation, she actually claps.

I know she's probably just encouraging me to keep going after my setback, but I appreciate it anyway. Having someone in your corner makes all the difference.

By Sunday, I'm feeling good about life. Work is getting better, I don't have to deal with my parents this weekend, I cancelled that stupid date with David, and the new dress I bought yesterday — a barely-there metallic bronze number that clings to every curve — is definitely going to knock Nils's socks off.

And hopefully convince him to come to the orgy at Chained tonight. It's a club I've been to before but don't frequent. More importantly, that means Brody won't be there. Maybe that will help Nils relax into the experience.

I arrive at Baltia around six, early enough that the club isn't open yet but late enough that Nils should be done with his paperwork. The side door is unlocked, so I let myself in and head toward his office.

But as I approach, I hear voices. His door is closed, which is unusual, and I can hear a female voice inside. Emma, maybe? It's hard to tell, muffled as it is by the thick wood.

"Oh my god," the voice groans, loud and unrestrained enough to be clear as day. And my blood turns to ice.

That was too loud to be an argument. In my not inconsiderable experience, that level of volume only comes from one thing. Pleasure. The kind of pleasure I know Nils can give. The kind of "oh my god" I myself have screamed for him before.

I turn on my heel and stride back toward the exit, my heels clicking angrily on the floor. But halfway there, I stop. No. I'm not running away. If it's what I think is happening, I deserve to look him in the eye when I kick his ass to the curb.

I march back to his office and raise my fist to bang on the door — but it flies open before I can. Emma pushes past me, her hair disheveled, her face flushed. She doesn't even acknowledge me, just continues down the hallway.

I look into the office to find Nils sitting behind

his desk, perfectly composed. Too composed. He rises when he sees me.

"Alexsis. You're early."

He moves to kiss me, but I step back. "What just happened?"

A pause. A purse of his lips. As if he's thinking up an excuse.

"Emma and I were having a private conversation."

"A conversation?" I can hear the skepticism in my own voice.

"Mostly fighting, actually. She's still upset about ... past incidents." He shrugs nonchalantly. He's either a really good actor ... or he's telling the truth.

"It sounded like there was something sexual going on," I say with the accusatory tone the words deserve.

His brows furrow. "There wasn't. Emma was upset about division of duties and got rather vocal about it."

"Her hair was a mess."

"She runs her hands through it when she's agitated." He tilts his head. "Are you jealous?"

The question hits too close to home. Because yes, I realize with a sinking feeling, I am jealous. Irrationally, possessively jealous. But I can't admit that. Not when I'm the one who keeps pushing for openness, for sexual freedom. Though that's supposed to come with the other's approval, and, by his request, their presence as well. Still, even the idea that he might be fucking her — or anyone else — brought out the worst in me.

"Of course not," I lie. "I just don't like being lied to."

Something flashes in his eyes — hurt, maybe. "I'm not lying to you."

The tension between us is palpable as we leave for dinner at the nearby Lemon Grove. Its rooftop views are spectacular, the city spreading out below us as the sun sets, but I can barely appreciate it. I keep replaying the scene in my mind. Emma's flushed face. The closed, *locked* door. That groan.

"The salmon is excellent here," Nils says, clearly trying to break through my mood.

"Mmm." I pretend to study the menu, but the words blur together.

"Alexsis." His hand covers mine on the table. "Nothing happened with Emma. I hope you can believe that."

I look up at him, wanting to believe. His ice-blue eyes are earnest, concerned. Maybe I'm being paranoid. Maybe the stress of everything is making me see things that aren't there.

"Okay," I say finally. "I believe you." And maybe I do. I want to, I realize.

The relief on his face makes me relax just a fraction. But my chest still feels tight with anxiety.

We manage to get through dinner with lighter conversation, but the earlier tension still hums beneath the surface.

As we leave the restaurant, Nils asks, "Would you like to see a movie? I'm in the mood for something relaxing."

"Does an orgy sound relaxing?" The words are out before I can stop them.

He chuckles, but it sounds forced. "Not particularly. But it's not out of the question."

"There's one tonight at a different club — Chained. Brody won't be there."

He considers this. "I'll go on one condition — we go to a movie another night. There's an independent film at the Nuart I'd really like to see."

"Deal." I smile, hoping it'll reassure him. I'm beyond relieved that he agreed to go to the orgy with me. Because I need it right now.

The ride to Chained is quiet. I fidget with the hem

of my dress, second-guessing everything. Maybe this is a bad idea. Maybe we should just go home, talk things through. But it's the only way I know to move past the uncertainty … and then we're pulling up to the club, and it's too late to change course.

The moment we walk into the orgy room, I realize I forgot to tell Nils that it's a BDSM club … though he might have already picked up on it from the name. If he didn't, the deep red walls adorned with various restraints and implements, and the clientele dressed in leather and latex just clued him in.

"Interesting," Nils murmurs, taking it all in.

A glance down at the bulge in his pants tells me he's into it.

I reach out and run my hand over the hard length. "Can I tie you up?" I ask with a raised brow.

He smirks. "Only if I can peel that sinfully tempting dress off of you first," he murmurs, teasing the hem with his fingers.

A shiver rolls through me, and I nod.

He grips the shimmering fabric, slowly sliding his hand up my inner thigh, using his thumb to brush my sex as he goes. Then grazing a nipple as he passes. Then using it to pin my arms over my head, my eyes covered, my mouth exposed. He uses it like a mask, gripping it behind my head so I can't move, pressing me into the wall behind us.

"We didn't talk about our boundaries," Nils murmurs against my lips. "But I'm at least going to need your safe word, love."

I bite into my lip as a surge of heat flows through me. "Sluta," I respond, having already looked up the word in anticipation of surprising him.

He chuckles, low and dark. "Learning Swedish, are we?" He audibly draws in a breath. "You're killing me, you know."

I grin, flicking my tongue in what I think is his direction.

"Let me resurrect you, then."

He groans and his mouth is on mine, hot and hard and demanding. And then in one swift motion he pulls back and finishes removing my dress, revealing his naked body, his hard cock standing at attention.

I raise an impressed eyebrow. "You're sneaky, I'll give you that." I grab his cock and use it to force him against the wall, then clip him into the restraints and step back.

I tap my finger against my chin, turning to survey the room.

I lock eyes with a blonde taking it up the ass from a large, muscled and masked man while another works the clamps on her nipples. She licks her lips at me and winks. I beckon with a finger in response. At her signal, both men stop, and all three approach.

I hear Nils buck against the wall. "What are you going to do, Tessa?" he taunts.

I look over my shoulder and wiggle my ass at him. "I'm going to make you watch," I reply lightly.

Mr. Muscles fists his cock and grins. I pull the blonde to me by her nipple clamps and kiss her, our tongues mingling as both men place themselves behind us.

I pull away. "Ah ah ah." I wiggle a finger. "Spankings first."

Both men eagerly snatch the nearest paddles, and Blondie and I tongue fuck as they start to spank us. After a few good hits, my pussy is dripping wet and Nils is groaning, his cock weeping. I break away and step up to him, lightly scratching up his cock. He hisses as I lean down, purposely displaying my wet pussy to the trio while my mouth hovers at Nils's cock.

I'm so focused that I don't even know who it is approaching, but a massive cock shoves into me from behind, pushing me forward onto Nils's erection. The head of his cock hits the back of my throat and Nils curses. I groan purposefully, the vibration driving him to thrust wildly. The cock inside me thrusts just as wildly as a hand smacks my ass hard. As I'm fucked into oblivion. As I take Nils's cock down my throat.

Someone attaches clamps to my nipples, and I cry out, Nils's cock spilling from my mouth when I do. He gasps in protest.

"Don't stop," he pleads, breathless.

I look up at him as mind numbing pleasure and pain rip through me. As Blondie lays beside me, working my nipple clamps while the guy who was working hers fucks her until her tits shake. Which must mean Mr. Muscles is fucking me.

Fucking me so good. So deep. So hard. I'm so close to coming.

But he's not as good as Nils, who continues to beg for release.

"Give me that mouth, Tessa," he pleads. "I want to come in that mouth."

"I want to come in that mouth *please*, *Mistress Tessa*," I correct.

He bucks against his restraints, trying to shove his cock back into my mouth. He must be so turned on he can't think straight. The realization makes me even wetter.

"On second thought, I don't think you deserve to come yet, brat," I tell him.

I pull off the cock that was inside me, turning my ass to Nils and rubbing up and down him, then sinking my soaked pussy onto his cock. I gesture for Mr. Muscles to come forward.

"Now, Mistress Tessa wants you both to fuck me until I come. And then you can come inside me like good boys," I direct sternly.

"Yes, Mistress Tessa," they say in unison. I arch in pleasure as Nils starts to fuck me like a wild animal from behind while I'm simultaneously fucked in the mouth. It's not long before they both blow their loads, hot cum filling me up from both ends. I thrash and writhe and come so hard while their hot seed spills into and out of my holes. They disobeyed me, but fuck if I care right now. This is my church. This is my religion. I have a purpose, a calling, to bring and receive pleasure. And I've only just begun.

I right myself, cum dripping down my chin and inner thigh as I release Nils. He pounces, driving me to the floor and fucking me hard and fast with his waning erection.

"You're going to pay for that," he growls in my ear. "I'm *your* master now."

He hauls back up and reaches for the restraints built into the floor around us, handcuffing me down spread eagle. He walks a circle around me, surveying me as he eyes a rack of hard-core-looking sex toys. Chains. Whips. And humongous dildos. He grabs one of those and sprays it down before wiping it off and mounting it in a strap-on harness above his actual cock. He gestures Blondie and the guy she'd been fucking to join us.

"I want you to sit on her face and let her eat you out," he directs Blondie. "And you —" he pulls the man toward him "— can fuck me while she watches."

My pussy clenches at his dirty commands. "I thought you were a top?"

He smirks at me. "Normally I am, but you wanted to see me with a man, didn't you?" I bite my lip and nod eagerly. "Yes, please, master," he commands.

"Yes, please, master," I parrot breathlessly.

"Good girl," he praises me, dropping to his knees between my legs. "As a reward, I'll fuck you with this until I can take you properly."

"While he fucks you?"

Nils grins as he hauls my legs up by the knees,

raising my hips to his and spearing me with the dildo. It's so huge I gasp at the intrusion. Thankfully, he supports my hips so I can have a moment to get used to it. Or so I think, until the guy lays down behind Nils, his massive, erect cock waiting. Nils lowers down enough to spear the waiting cock, groaning as it slides into his ass. And then he positions me carefully so every time he works over the cock in his ass, he pumps in and out of me on the dildo.

It's like nothing I've ever experienced. My entire body feels like it's on fire with need as I watch Nils fuck us both. I'm a wet, whimpering mess, climbing to peaks I never even knew existed before … and then Blondie's dripping pussy is in my face.

I groan, and let her ride my face, licking and sucking as I'm fucked, listening to the sounds of two sets of balls slapping, feeling the massive dildo stimulate the deep nerves of my G-spot.

The hedonistic symphony of flesh and moans, not just from us but the entire room — slapping and spanking and fucking and screaming — I come apart at the seams over and over again. Blondie with me as she finds her pleasure on my tongue.

Then Nils pulls out and lowers my hips.

"Come on her," I hear him say. And then the dildo slides back in as the guy who was fucking him comes into view, his cock red, aching, and ready to spill.

"On my tits," I beg.

He leans forward, rips off the condom he was wearing, and lets Blondie suck him almost to completion before pulling out of her mouth and coming all over both of our tits. And as he does, Nils fucks me hard and fast. And I come, shattering, spent, and utterly sated in a way I've never been before.

Blondie leans down and kisses me languidly before she and her man toy wander off to find their next pleasure.

Nils lifts me in his arms, leaning us against the wall. He offers me a water bottle I have no idea how he got but I drink greedily, nonetheless.

I give Nils a sex-soaked smile and wrap my legs around his middle, sitting up in his lap.

"That was — without exaggeration — the most insane, intense sexual experience of my entire life," I admit.

He kisses me softly on the lips. "After all the orgies I've been part of, I didn't think anything could surprise me," he responds. "But honestly, it was for me, too."

The way he looks at me takes my breath away.

And I hear the words he doesn't say. The ones that I'm thinking. It's because of him. I've never experienced this before because I wasn't with him. With someone who understands me. Who is on my level. Who wants to please me. Tease me. Fuck me. And care for me. I'm not a hole to be filled. I'm not a plaything to discard. Somehow, even with all of the uncertainty in my life, our lives, we've managed to form a bond of trust.

My insides clench … this time in fear. Even though this is what I've been looking for all my life, now that I've found it … well, I know I can't keep it. I know I'll be forced to choose.

And I'll choose wrong.

It's what I do.

I chose porn to pay for college instead of simply admitting that my part time job wasn't cutting it and getting loans.

I choose to lie to my parents over and over. Going to church every Sunday, pretending to share their faith. Dating the never-ending parade of good Mormon boys they tried to entice me into marrying.

I choose to use sex to cover up the serious emotional damage of my childhood.

I'm just about to share that particular revelation

when a familiar voice behind me says, "I thought I might find you here."

Nils and I freeze at the same time. There's anger in his eyes. And I'm sure there's fear in mine.

I turn to find Brody grinning at us.

"I thought you said he wouldn't be here," Nils says in a tone low enough for only me to hear.

"I thought he wouldn't." I rise and face Brody. "What are you doing here?"

His grin turns feline, and he steps forward, giving my nipple a cheeky pinch. "I'm here for the orgy, of course. Why else would I be here?" He looks to Nils. "I saw you topping as a bottom. Nice."

Nils huffs, rising and disengaging the strap-on harness, letting it drop to the floor. His hand wraps around me from behind, splaying possessively over my stomach.

And something about the gesture rubs me the wrong way. Like he's staking out his territory. Like I'm his property. I step away. Toward Brody.

"Mm," Brody murmurs. "Down to play after all, Tessa?" He steps forward to meet me.

"Tessa," Nils says tightly from behind me.

Brody grins and leans in. "You gonna let lover boy tell you who to fuck?" He reaches down and strokes me exactly the way he knows will make me wet for him. I arch mindlessly toward him.

Nils physically puts himself between Brody and me, pushing Brody backward.

"Are you really going to fuck him? Stop and think," he says firmly, his eyes full of angry fire. "He's practically stalking you. He's clearly obsessed with you. Isn't it obvious?"

"Maybe," I allow, stroking a hand down his chest. "Is it wrong that I'm incredibly turned on by your jealousy, though?"

Nils's lips set in a thin line. "You think I'm jealous of him?"

I step forward. "If you're telling me who I can and cannot fuck … then yes, I'd say that makes you jealous."

He clenches his jaw so tight I see the muscle flutter. "I'm not telling you who you can fuck. I'm simply telling you what I see."

I tilt my head, already knowing I'm going to push. And hating myself for it. "So if I fucked him in front of you. Let him fill me up with his cum while you watched … that wouldn't make you jealous?" My hand wraps around his cock and tugs. Unbelievably, he hardens at my touch. I look up at him from under my eyelashes. "You like watching someone fuck me, don't you, baby?"

His nostrils flare. "I like it better when I'm calling the shots. When I'm the reason you're coming, even if it's on someone else's cock."

I suck in a sharp breath as desire shoots through me. Why do I need to feel like I'm doing something wrong to get that rush?

"Then tell me how to fuck him."

Nils steps forward. And while he's usually so calm, there's a tension in him now that makes me take a step back. "Stop this. Anyone but him." He gestures around. "There's a room full of cocks, including mine. But that's not enough for you. Do you truly have to get off on the one you know will hurt me the most? Is that what gets you off? Controlling me? Hurting me?"

His words hit too close to home. Because on some level … I know he's right. But at the same time, it feels like he's wrong.

"Aren't you the one controlling me here?" I snap back. "I don't have feelings for him. It's just sex. Can't you trust that? Like I trust that you weren't fucking Emma?"

Nils gives a sharp, cutting laugh. "You're not going to back down on this, I can see that. Fine. I guess it's not fair to ask you to, considering this was the deal from the start. You were perfectly up front about the fact that you want to be able to fuck who you want, when you want. You go fuck Brody and I'll —"

"Go fuck another woman to make me jealous, too?" I resist the urge to clap a hand over my mouth once the words are out.

Nils's expression falls, the fire banking only to be replaced with disappointment. A look I know well. "No, Alexsis," he says quietly. "I would never do that to you. And I thought this thing between us, whatever it is, meant enough to you …" He trails off, shaking his head. "Never mind. Fuck him if that's what you really want. But I won't be staying to watch."

He turns and collects his clothes.

Before I know it, he's walking away.

I watch, my heart shattering with each step he takes. I instinctually move to follow him, but Brody's hand lands on my shoulder.

"Let him go," he says softly. "He can't give you what you need. But I can."

I turn to look at him, this man who's been a constant in my chaotic life. Who never judges, never asks for more than I can give. Who doesn't make me feel like I'm too much or not enough. Even if it's only flesh deep, I've always taken what he has to give, knowing I don't deserve more.

That's why I push Nils away. That's why I tested him. Because I know I don't deserve him. But Brody? He's as messed up as I am. Because Nils can not only give me what I need, he can also give me what I want. What I know I don't deserve. And Nils … he deserves better than me. So maybe it's better if I do let him go.

"Okay," I whisper, even as emptiness spreads through my chest.

He leads me to the wall, and I let him restrain me, touch me, move me, fill me. But it's mechanical now. My body responds out of habit, but my mind is elsewhere. On Nils walking away. On the hurt in his eyes. On the realization that I sabotaged the best thing in my life because I'm too broken to let go of my fear long enough to accept real intimacy.

When it's over, I slide back into my dress and turn to Brody.

"Why did you come here tonight?" I ask quietly. Hoping with Nils gone, he'll give me a real answer this time.

"I heard you might be here," he admits, rolling his eyes to play off the implications of that.

His answer should make me feel something. But I'm numb.

"From who?" I ask, mostly out of curiosity.

He doesn't answer, and I'm too tired to push. Too tired to do anything but wonder why I'm like this. Why I can't just be normal. Why I push away everyone who tries to really care about me.

"I should go," I say finally.

"Come on, Tessa, stay. All you need is a good spanking and you'll be right as rain," he says with a wink.

"No thanks. See you around, Brody."

I shake my head sadly as I leave. Because what I really need is to go home and figure out why I'm so broken. And how to fix it. How to fix what I have — had? — with Nils. If it can even be fixed at all.

When I get home, I take a long, hot shower. I may have let Brody fuck me, but it's Nils that I still smell all over me. And it's leaving me choking on regret. As I soap myself off and return to my own smell of jasmine-scented body wash, I reflect on the day. A day that started so promising. Things have been better at work —

I gasp as it hits me. Too many thoughts at once. I shave my legs as I untangle them.

I went after that record label article because I

reacted emotionally. Max and West were upset, and the unfairness of it all seemed too great to let slide. But eventually I realized Jason was right; I needed to check myself. To focus on reality, even if it was hard to admit that I can't take on every fight and win. I mastered myself, apologized, and accepted what I needed to do to make things right. To pursue my goals in a way that wasn't self-sabotaging.

Which means I can do that with my personal life, too. I think. Maybe … because my personal life is an emotional mess. A puzzle I clearly don't feel like I deserve to solve. To have the life I choose. To have love. Maybe that's because it's been denied to me by the people who were supposed to give it freely; my parents.

Maybe that's why I've been looking for validation in all the ways they told me were sinful to find it. My own career. Pleasures of the flesh. Love outside of marriage.

I've pursued them all trying to fill the hole the absence of their love left. The problem with that? Turns out it's more like a black hole, sucking up everything I throw into it and using it to grow.

Maybe I need to stop trying to fill that hole. Maybe I need to deal with it instead.

I fall asleep that night, tears staining my pillow,

with no plan but at least with a deeper understanding of how I got here. And the desire to break this pattern of ignoring my pain and keeping people at arm's length with all of my secrets and lies. At least I've stopped lying to myself. It's a good first step in the right direction.

19

───────

NILS

The morning light filtering through my bedroom window feels like an accusation. I've been staring at the ceiling for hours, replaying last night on an endless loop. The orgy. Brody. Walking away from Alexsis.

Did she fuck him?

The thought sends another wave of nausea through me, adding to the cocktail of regret that's been churning in my stomach since I left that club. I shouldn't have agreed to go. I should have seen it coming when she was already on edge about Emma. I should have stayed and fought for her instead of walking away like a coward.

But watching her step toward him, seeing that self-destructive glint in her eyes ... I couldn't do it. I couldn't stand there and watch her use sex with Brody as another way to push me away.

Did she fuck him?

I throw off the covers and head for the shower, cranking it as hot as it'll go. Maybe if I scald myself enough, I can burn away the image of her arching toward his touch. The memory of her asking if I'd fuck another woman to make her jealous, as if I could ever —

No. I'm not doing this. I have three clubs to run and dwelling on what may or may not have happened after I left isn't going to change anything.

By seven a.m., I'm at Baltia, a full three hours before I need to be. The empty club feels appropriate somehow — all that space meant for pounding music, sweating bodies, and visceral connection, echoing with nothing but my footsteps. I head straight for the stockroom and start doing inventory. Counting bottles is mindless enough that I can almost pretend my chest doesn't feel like it's been hollowed out.

I move on to checking the sound equipment, then reviewing the bar setup, then organizing the office supplies. Anything to keep my hands busy and my mind occupied. It works, mostly. Except for when I find one of Alexsis's hair ties behind my desk. Or when I catch a whiff of jasmine from god knows where — probably a figment of my masochistic imagination. Or when I realize I'm checking my phone every five minutes even though she hasn't texted.

Did she fuck him?

"You look like shit."

I glance up from the spreadsheet I've been staring at without seeing to find Frankie settling into the chair across from my desk. Julian looms behind her, arms crossed over his massive chest.

"Thanks," I mutter, turning back to my computer. "What are you doing here so early?"

"Emma called. Said you two had another blow-up yesterday, so I came to talk." Frankie leans back, studying me. "But now I'm more curious about why you look like someone killed your dog."

"I don't have a dog."

"Nils."

I sigh and save the spreadsheet before meeting her eyes. "Emma and I did have a fight. She's upset that I ordered supplies for Allure along with the other clubs. Apparently, I should be leaving her club alone and letting her run it as she sees fit."

Julian snorts. "Her club?"

"That's what I said. Well, more or less. I told her

she may manage it, but she's still under my supervision." I run a hand through my hair. "Still, I apologized for overstepping, but she just kept yelling. Something about me undermining her authority."

"And?" Frankie prompts, because of course she knows there's more.

"And she's smart. She's capable. She's proven she can do the job. She just needs to stop trying to assert her authority in these aggressive bids to prove herself. There's no need for it."

"Interesting perspective," a voice says to my right.

I turn to find Emma standing in my doorway, and my stomach drops. "How long have you been there?"

"The whole time," Frankie says cheerfully. "I asked her to wait outside and listen. Figured it would be more honest this way."

I shoot Frankie a look that she completely ignores as Emma enters the office, closing the door behind her.

"I'm sorry," Emma says, and I can see she means it. "You're right. I have been trying too hard to prove myself. I've been taking business classes, learning everything I can, trying so hard to act like the boss that I forgot that being bossy isn't the same as being a leader."

"Exactly," Julian says, surprising all of us. He's usually content to let Frankie handle the talking. "Look at Nils. He's the most laid-back dude I've ever seen, and he runs everything perfectly. Three clubs, and barely a hiccup. You don't have to be a hard-ass to be in charge."

I stare at Julian, genuinely shocked by the praise. He's not exactly free with compliments.

He shrugs. "What? It's true."

Emma turns back to me. "Would you be willing to give me another shot? I promise to dial back the attitude and actually listen when you're trying to help."

"Of course," I say, meaning it. "We all have learning curves."

She moves toward me, arms opening for a hug, and I hold up a hand. She freezes, hurt flashing across her face.

"Under normal circumstances, I'd be happy to hug it out," I explain quickly. "But Alexsis already thinks we were fucking yesterday when we were actually fighting. I don't want to do anything that could be misconstrued."

Understanding dawns in Emma's eyes. "Oh god, is that why she — I wondered why she looked ready to murder me when I passed her in the hall." She winces. "Do you want me to talk to her? Explain that nothing happened?"

The offer is tempting, but I shake my head. "I appreciate it, but I wouldn't ask you to get in the middle of this."

Emma nods. "Well, if you change your mind ... I know we haven't exactly been besties lately, but I don't want to cause problems for you two."

I give her a vague smile in response and after an awkward pause, Frankie gestures for her to leave.

After she's gone, Frankie and Julian exchange a look.

"You want to talk about what's really going on?" Frankie asks gently.

"Not particularly."

"Too bad." She leans forward. "Spill."

I debate refusing, but the weight of last night is crushing me. "Alexsis and I went to an orgy last night. Everything was fine until Brody showed up."

"Brody?" Julian asks.

"Some fuck boy she has history with. He's obsessed with her, and she ..." I trail off, not sure how to explain the dynamic. "She wanted to fuck him. I didn't want her to. So, I walked away."

Frankie's eyebrows climb. "You just left?"

"What was I supposed to do? Stand there and

watch her self-destruct? Watch her fuck him just to prove she could?" The words come out harsher than intended. "She accused me of being controlling, of being jealous."

"Are you jealous?" Frankie asks.

I consider lying, but what's the point? "Of course I am. But it's more than that. She uses sex like a weapon — against herself more than anyone. And Brody ... he enables it. He shows up wherever she is, he pushes her buttons, and she lets him because it's easier than dealing with whatever she's actually feeling."

"So, you walked away," Julian says. It's not a judgment, just a statement.

"I walked away." The admission sits heavy in the room. "And now I can't stop wondering if she actually went through with it."

"Does it matter?" Frankie asks.

I look at her sharply. "Of course it matters."

"Why? If she did fuck him, it's because she's spiraling. If she didn't, she's still spiraling. Either way, the question is what you're going to do about it."

I slump back in my chair. "Nothing. There's nothing to do. She made her choice."

"Did she? Or did she just do what she probably

always does when someone gets too close?" Frankie's voice is gentle but pointed. "Look, I don't know Alexsis that well, but I know self-sabotage when I see it … or hear it. You know what I mean. Anyway. What I also know is *you*. You don't give up on people you care about."

"Maybe I should start."

Julian laughs, a short bark of sound. "Right. Because that's worked so well for you in the past."

I glare at him, but he's unmoved.

"Come on, man. You carried a torch for Frankie for how long? And when that didn't work out, you threw yourself even deeper into this job, pretending like it never happened. Now you've finally found someone who actually wants you back, who's into all the same kinky shit you are, and you're going to give up because she's got issues?"

"We all have issues," Frankie adds. "The question is whether she's worth fighting through them."

Is she?

I think about Alexsis laughing at the diner, her eyes bright with mischief. The way she looks at me when we're alone, like I'm something precious. How right it feels when she's in my arms, even when everything else is chaos.

"She's worth it," I admit quietly. "But I can't be the only one fighting."

Frankie reaches across the desk and squeezes my hand. "Then give her a chance to fight, too. But first, maybe give both of you some time to cool off."

After they leave, I try to go back to work, but the spreadsheet might as well be hieroglyphics. I close my laptop and lean back, staring at the ceiling.

Did she fuck him?

I realize Frankie is right; it might not matter. What matters is that we're both hurting, both stuck in patterns we can't seem to break. Her with her self-destruction, me with my walking away.

Maybe Frankie's right. Maybe we both need time to figure out if we're willing to fight for this.

I pull out my phone and stare at our message thread. The last text from her was about meeting at the club yesterday. Before everything went to hell.

I don't type anything. Not yet. But for the first time since walking out of that club, I let myself hope that this isn't the end.

20

———

ALEXSIS

I'm in the conference room, elbow-deep in research on the underground music scene in Koreatown when someone clears their throat above me. I look up, expecting Max to have returned with lunch, but find Emma standing there instead. My stomach immediately clenches.

"Can we talk?" she asks, and there's something in her expression that stops me from telling her to fuck off.

"I guess," I say warily, gesturing to Max's empty chair.

Emma sits, smoothing her hands over her shorts. Gone is the leather-clad manager who caught Nils and me in her office. This Emma looks ... normal.

Human, even in a knee-length jean cutoffs with a black tank top.

"I wanted to clear something up," she starts. "About yesterday, with Nils."

My jaw tightens. "I don't really want to hear —"

"Nothing happened." She says it firmly, meeting my eyes. "We were fighting about work stuff. I was being a bitch about him ordering supplies for my club. That's it."

I study her face, looking for the lie. "His door was locked."

"I did that. I didn't want anyone to walk in on us so I could give him a piece of my mind, uninterrupted. I was pissed off and combative, and it was dumb." She laughs, but it's self-deprecating. "Anyway. I'm actually seeing someone. Have been for a couple of months now. I assure you I have absolutely no interest in Nils, nor he in me, and there was definitely not anything sexual going on in that office. Unless he gets off on being told he's an idiot by a former hairdresser who's attempting to be a club manager. Doing a bang-up job, too, aren't I?" She rolls her eyes, clearly at herself.

She's so real, it's hard not to believe her. The knot in my chest loosens slightly, but I'm not ready to let my guard down completely. "Why did you feel the need to come here and tell me all this?"

Emma leans back, considering. "Because I've known Nils for a while now. I was there when he was hung up on Frankie." My eyebrows shoot up, and she nods. "Yeah, I knew. I kept my mouth shut because it wasn't my business. But my point is, I've never seen him like this before. The way he is with you."

"Like what?" The words come out smaller than I intended.

"Serious. Real. Completely fucking gone for you." She tilts her head to the side and gives me a small, pitying smile.

Nils is gone for me? I find it hard to believe, but ... then, why else would he keep sticking around? She's right. He must be. And I didn't even realize it.

The tears come before I can stop them. Because that just makes it worse. Nils is incredible — patient, understanding, sexy as hell — and I'm the disaster who accused him of lying, who pushed him away, who chose to hurt him rather than deal with my own shit.

"Hey," Emma says softly, pulling tissues from her purse. "It's okay."

"It's not okay," I manage between sobs. "I'm horrible. The way I've treated him ..."

Emma scoots her chair closer. "You want to talk about it?"

And for some reason — maybe because she's practically a stranger, maybe because I'm at rock bottom — I tell her everything. About my family, about the double life, about Brody and the sex clubs and how I use it all to keep people at a distance. About how I pushed Nils away because I don't know how to let anyone really love me, because deep down I think I don't deserve it.

Emma listens without judgment, occasionally making sympathetic noises. When I finally run out of words and tears, she hands me another tissue.

"You want my advice on how to fix it?" she asks.

I laugh, but it's watery. "I'm a sobbing mess, at *work* no less. So yeah, I'll take whatever I can get to get off this ride."

"Talk to him. Be honest. Tell him what you just told me." She shrugs. "He's a reasonable guy, and he obviously cares about you. Sometimes the simplest solution is the right one."

"You make it sound so easy."

"It's simple, yes, but not easy. It's worth it, though, don't you think?"

I nod, wiping my eyes. "It is. You're right. Thank you. For this. For coming here. You didn't have to."

"Yeah, well." Emma stands, looking slightly embarrassed by the emotional moment. "Us fuck-ups have to stick together, right?"

I surprise us both by standing and hugging her. She's stiff for a moment before returning it.

"Good luck," she says as she pulls away. "And Alexsis? Don't wait too long. Guys like Nils ... they don't come around often."

After she leaves, I sit back down and stare at my computer screen without seeing it. My phone buzzes — a text from Max explaining our order took longer than she thought it would and that she's finally headed back. I unlock my phone to text her back when I notice the missed call notification.

My parents.

With trembling fingers, I listen to the voicemail.

"Alexsis, this is your father." His voice is cold, clipped. "We've been waiting for you to call and explain yourself for missing lunch and canceling on David. A young man from a good family, and you couldn't even give him the courtesy of meeting him. Your mother is beside herself. We expect you to call back immediately."

I delete the voicemail and set my phone aside. Like that will make it go away. I know it won't, but I can't deal with them right now. Not when I have something more important to fix first.

Before I can lose my nerve, I pick up my phone again and call Nils.

He answers on the third ring. "Alexsis." Just my name, but I can hear the caution in his voice.

"Hey. I know I'm probably the last person you want to hear from right now, but … can we talk?" I ask. "In person? Please?"

A pause. "Yes, of course we can. When and where?"

"Tonight? You could come to my place?"

He sighs. "Okay. I'll be there at eight."

"Nils?" I say before he can hang up. "Thank you."

"Don't thank me yet," he says softly. "We've got a lot of shit to work through." And then he's gone.

AT SEVEN FORTY-FIVE, I'M PACING MY LIVING ROOM like a caged animal. I've changed outfits three times before settling on jeans and a simple white scoop-neck tee — this isn't about seduction. It's about honesty.

When the knock comes at exactly eight, my heart lodges in my throat. I open the door to find Nils standing there in dark designer jeans and a grey henley that hugs his lean, toned torso, hands shoved in his pockets. He looks tired and wary, but still so beautiful it makes my chest ache.

"Come in," I say, stepping back.

He follows me to the couch but doesn't sit until I do, leaving careful space between us.

"I'm sorry," I start, because that's the most important thing. "For last night. For pushing you. For accusing you of lying about Emma. For ... all of it."

He's quiet, watching me with those ice-blue eyes that see too much.

"I talked to Emma," I continue. "She came to see me at work. She told me nothing happened between you two."

"I told you that." He sounds more exhausted than chastising. I just hope I haven't exhausted his ability to forgive. God knows he's had to do a lot of that where I'm concerned.

"I know. I should have believed you. I just ..." I take a shaky breath. "I've been doing a lot of thinking. About why I am the way I am. Why I push people away. Why I sabotage anything good in my life."

"And?"

That one syllable gives me hope. And the

courage to keep going. Because at least he's not shutting me down. He's hearing me out. So, I meet his eyes.

"I think I've been trying to fill this hole inside me. The one my parents created with their conditional love, their expectations, their making me feel like who I am is shameful. And I've been filling it with sex and secrets and anything that lets me feel in control. But it just makes the hole bigger."

Nils shifts slightly closer. "Go on."

"You scare me," I admit. "Because you see me. The real me. And you don't run away. You don't try to fix me or change me. You just ... accept me. And I don't know how to handle that because I've never had it before."

"Alexsis —"

"I'm not done." I need to get this out before I lose my nerve. "I want to change. Not for you, but for me. Because I'm tired of being two different people. I'm tired of pushing away anyone who tries to care about me. I'm tired of being afraid."

My voice cracks on the last word, and suddenly Nils is pulling me into his arms. I bury my face in his chest, breathing in his familiar scent.

"I care about you," I whisper. "So much it terrifies me."

He pulls back enough to look at me. "I care about you, too. I'm falling for you, Alexsis. Hard."

"Even after everything?" I ask doubtfully.

"Because of everything." He cups my face in his hands. "You have such fire, such strength. You've been fighting this battle alone for so long, but you don't have to do it by yourself anymore. I'm here. If you'll let me be."

"I don't know how to do this," I admit. "How to be in a real relationship. How to be vulnerable."

He huffs out a dry laugh. "I can't exactly say I'm great at it either. But we'll figure it out together."

Together. The word splits my heart open, in the best way. I kiss him then, soft and sweet, trying to pour all the things I can't say yet into the contact. When we break apart, I rest my forehead against his.

"Can we just ... be normal for a while?" I ask. "Date like regular people? No sex clubs, no games, just us?"

A smile tugs at his lips. "I'd like that."

So we order takeout and watch a movie, curled together on my couch like any normal couple. And I invite him to stay the night. I let him undress me, lay me down on the bed. And he takes me, missionary style. Something I'd previously considered boring, vanilla. But with Nils? It could never be either. He arouses parts of me, physically and emotionally, that no one ever has. Every touch, every moan, every thrust is so much *more* than it's ever been. And when we come apart together, it's with an intimacy that doesn't need kinky positions, restraints, or lubricated toys; just the connection between us.

THE NEXT TWO WEEKS ARE THE HAPPIEST I CAN remember. We see that indie film at the Nuart that Nils wanted to watch — a moody Swedish drama that I pretend to understand but mostly just enjoy observing his face as he watches. We go to an art gallery opening in Silver Lake where Nils surprises me with his knowledge of contemporary photography. We pack a picnic for a concert at the Hollywood Bowl, lying on a blanket under the stars while the LA Philharmonic plays.

It's all the wholesome dating I used to have to fake with the Mormon boys my parents threw at me, but with the crucial difference that I actually want to be here. That when Nils settles behind me and wraps me in his arms during the concert, my whole body sighs with contentment. That when we go back to his place or mine afterward, the sex is mind-blowing because it's real, it's us, and it's not about pushing boundaries, proving anything, or hiding from my emotions.

I don't miss the sex clubs. I don't miss Brody. I don't miss any of it, because what I have with Nils is so much better. He makes me laugh. He challenges me intellectually. He supports my career ambitions and listens to my article ideas with genuine interest. And the sex ... god, the sex is better than ever because there's trust there now. Real trust.

I'm in the middle of transcribing an interview on a Tuesday afternoon when my phone rings. The display shows a number I don't recognize, but something makes me answer anyway.

"Alexsis? It's Frankie Greco."

I straighten in my chair. "Oh, hi. Is everything okay? Is Nils —"

"He's fine," she says quickly. "But I am calling about him. It's his birthday tomorrow."

"What?" I practically shriek, then lower my voice when Max looks over. "He didn't tell me."

"Of course he didn't. He never makes a big deal about it. Which is why I forgot, too, what with the kids and the pregnancy — oh shit, you didn't know about that either. It's kind of still supposed to be a secret." She sighs.

"Congratulations," I say, laughing. "I promise I won't say anything."

"Thanks. Anyway, I want to throw him a surprise party at the club tomorrow night. Think you can keep him busy until we're ready?"

"Absolutely."

"Great. I'll text you when we're set up. Probably around nine?"

"Sounds good."

After we hang up, I immediately text Nils asking if he can meet me for dinner tomorrow night near my work — far enough from Baltia to keep him well away from the preparations — to discuss something important. He agrees, though I can read his concern in his texts. I smile, knowing for once it's going to be a *good* surprise.

WEDNESDAY EVENING, I'M A BUNDLE OF NERVES AS Nils walks into the restaurant. He looks gorgeous in slim-fit tailored black slacks and a light blue button-down. But there's worry in his eyes as he slides into the booth across from me.

We order — pasta for me, steak for him — and

make small talk until the food arrives. Finally, he can't take it anymore.

"What's this important thing you wanted to discuss?" he asks carefully. "Is everything okay?"

I put on my best stern face. "Actually, I'm very upset with you."

He pales slightly. "What did I do?"

"It's what you didn't do. You didn't tell me it was your birthday."

His shoulders relax, and he actually laughs. "How did you find out?"

Time for my acting skills. "I saw your driver's license when you pulled it out at the liquor store the other day."

"Ah." He looks sheepish. "Well, I don't really like making a big deal about it." He shrugs.

"Would it be making too big a deal to get a special dessert to celebrate?" I ask, letting my stern expression soften. "And then maybe I can be your dessert later?"

His eyes darken. "I'm definitely okay with that."

We return to normal chatter over dinner, then share a ridiculous chocolate lava cake that's more chocolate than cake for dessert. I'm licking fudge off my spoon in a way that has Nils shifting in his seat when my phone buzzes. I pull it out subtly to see a text from Frankie.

All ready!

I type back that we're almost done, and thirty seconds later, Nils's phone rings.

"Frankie?" He frowns. "What's wrong?"

I can hear her panicked voice from across the table. Something about missing equipment. Nils sighs and hangs up, giving me a wary look.

"Frankie needs me to stop by Baltia for a few minutes. Some crisis with equipment. I don't know what she's freaking out over, because there's nothing going on tonight at any of the clubs. But she says jump …" I nod in understanding. "Do you mind?"

"Of course not," I say, fighting a smile. "Let's go. The sooner we get it over with, the sooner you get second dessert." I wink at him, and if I'm not mistaken, he moves just a bit faster.

It doesn't take long to get there and the club is suspiciously dark when we arrive. I have to bite my lip to keep from grinning as Nils uses his key to let us in.

"Frankie?" he calls. "Where —"

The lights flick on, revealing a good sized crowd of people who yell a chorus of "SURPRISE!"

Nils freezes, genuinely shocked as Frankie steps

forward with a huge grin, Julian and Emma flanking her. Behind them, I spot Max with West and the rest of Violent Mood Swings setting up on stage, and, of course, the whole other crowd of people, none of whom I recognize. I'm impressed that she got this many people to be quiet.

"Happy birthday, you Swedish bastard," Frankie says, pulling him into a hug.

Nils looks at me over her shoulder, and I shrug innocently. "You really thought I was going to let your birthday pass without celebrating?"

He extracts himself from Frankie and pulls me against his side. "You were in on this."

"Guilty," I admit with a sly smile.

"Unfortunately," Frankie interrupts, "the equipment emergency wasn't entirely fake. We really can't find the backup sound board, and the main one isn't working."

Nils sighs, but he's smiling. "I'm pretty sure I know where it is."

For the next hour, I get a front-row seat to Nils in his element. Turns out it wasn't where it was supposed to be, so he systematically searches the club, checks inventory logs and makes calls to the other clubs to see if it was misplaced. I trail after him, genuinely fascinated.

"How do you keep track of all this?" I ask as he cross-references serial numbers on his phone.

"Practice," he says, but he looks pleased by my interest. "Each piece of equipment has a code. Once you know the system ..."

He explains the coding system, and then, as we continue to search, he fills me in on other aspects of the job like tracking maintenance schedules, creating employee schedules, handling vendor relationships, and all the other million moving parts that keep a club running. I had no idea how much went into it beyond booking acts and serving drinks. I say as much to him, which the band hears. Wade even adds in that a good club manager knows all the up-and-coming bands, as well as the big ones, so their shows are always stacked with talent, adding that Nils is particularly good at that. I'm in awe. It's like club managers have to be an office manager, equipment manager, finance expert, music industry guru, and too many other roles to count.

And my man does this for a living.

He is so getting extra laid tonight. As if he wasn't already. It is his birthday, after all.

"Found it," Emma calls from the basement storage. "Someone put it behind the Halloween decorations."

"From last year?" Nils asks, incredulous. "When I find out who —"

"Hey, don't worry about it. Problem solved," Frankie says. "It's your birthday. Kick asses tomorrow, party now." She turns to Ace, the stage manager. "Let's get the band playing so the birthday boy can actually enjoy his party?" Ace nods and scurries off to do just that.

Minutes later, the band launches into their set, and I pull Nils onto the dance floor. It's different from the sweaty, sexual dancing at Los Jardines or Allure. This is pure joy, celebration, us moving together to music that feels like possibility.

"Thank you," he says during a slower song, pulling me close. "For this. For everything."

"This was all Frankie," I hedge.

He shakes his head. "I meant thank you for being here. With me. For being you."

I smile up at him, my heart brimming with happiness. "Thank you for being born," I reply, and he laughs.

"I love you," he says suddenly, and my heart stops.

I look up at him, seeing the truth of it in his eyes. And I want to say it back. I can feel the words on my tongue. But …

"I'm getting there," I say softly, honestly. "I can feel it happening. But I can't say it yet. I need to really know I feel it before I do."

He kisses me softly. "I wouldn't want you to say it for any other reason."

"Take me home?" I ask. "I want to give you your real present."

We make our excuses to Frankie, who waggles her eyebrows suggestively, and head back to his place. And if I can't say the words yet, I show him with my body, with my mouth, with every touch how much he means to me. I worship him the way he's worshipped me, taking my time, taking him apart piece by piece until he's gasping my name like a prayer.

After, lying tangled in his sheets, as I fall asleep in his arms, I think about how different this feels from before. There's no urgency to fill a void, no desperate need to prove something. Just us, just this, just the quiet certainty that we're building something real.

"Best birthday ever," he murmurs sleepily.

I smile against his skin. "Wait until you see what I do for thirty-six."

He laughs loudly, honestly, and there goes my

heart brimming with joy again. And maybe something more.

21

———

ALEXSIS

I'm still riding the high from Nils's birthday party when inspiration strikes Thursday morning. I'm at my desk, transcribing notes from the Korean underground music scene piece, when my mind keeps drifting back to watching Nils work. The way he'd handled the equipment crisis. Hearing about the complexities of all the many other tasks he handles. Wade's comment about how good managers know all the up-and-coming bands. How Frankie had pulled together that party on such short notice.

Club managers. The unseen architects of the rock world.

My fingers fly across the keyboard as I outline the article. How managers like Nils don't just book bands and count inventory — they shape careers. They give unknowns their first real stage. They create the environments where established acts can experiment. They're tastemakers, gatekeepers, and nurturers all rolled into one.

I'm so absorbed that I don't notice Jason approaching until he clears his throat.

"You look intense," he observes. "What's got you so focused?"

I spin my laptop toward him. "Article idea. The invisible influence of rock club managers. How they shape the industry from behind the scenes."

Jason's eyebrows rise as he scans my outline. "This is good. Really good. You have sources?"

"I can get them." I'm already mentally cataloging who to interview — Nils, obviously, but I'll need to be careful about bias. Frankie. Maybe some managers from The Roxy, The Viper Room, The Troubadour.

"Write it," Jason says. "If it's as good as this outline, it's your first byline."

My heart stops. "Really?"

"Really. Don't make me regret it."

I spend the week in a journalism fugue state. I barely see Nils — who is thankfully understanding and supportive of my need to focus, and also helps where he can — and I manage to interview eight different club managers, two booking agents, and a handful of musicians who credit specific venues with launching their careers. I'm careful to incorporate Nils's input objectively, just one voice among many, even though his insights are the most thoughtful, probably because he's comfortable being unguarded with me. Perks of the relationship, and I'm grateful for his help.

"It's about curation," he tells me during our formal interview, professional despite the fact that we'd been naked in his bed an hour earlier. "Anyone can book a band. But knowing which band to book on which night, how to build a lineup that creates energy, how to spot talent before they break — that's the art of it."

The article comes together like magic. I weave in stories of managers who championed acts that labels initially rejected, who created themed nights that became cultural movements, who turned struggling venues into institutions. By the time I submit it to Jason at the end of the week, I know it's good.

He calls me into his office the next Monday.

"Congratulations," he says, sliding a mockup

across his desk. "Your first byline. It'll be on the cover and everything."

And there it is, in bold swirling letters next to the issue's cover photo: "The Puppet Masters: How Rock's Club Managers Shape the Sound of a Generation." And on the inside mockup, the credit reads "by Alexsis Monaghan."

Not Alex M. Alexsis Monaghan.

I may actually cry.

Not here though.

"Thank you," I manage. "Thank you so much."

"You earned it. This is exactly the kind of piece I wanted from you — insightful, well-researched, a fresh angle on the industry." He leans back. "Keep this up and we'll talk about that promotion sooner rather than later."

I float out of his office. My first real byline. My name on a piece I'm genuinely proud of. Max stops me on the way to my desk to congratulate me and offers to take me out to lunch. I happily accept and head back to my desk. I'm reaching for my phone to text Nils when it buzzes with a voicemail notification.

My parents. Again.

The elation drains out of me as I listen to the voicemail.

"Alexsis Marie." My father's voice is steel. "Your behavior is absolutely unacceptable. Three weeks of silence. Ignoring our calls. Your mother is beside herself."

There's a shuffle, then my mother's voice, thick with tears. "What did we do wrong, sweetheart? Why are you punishing us like this? All we've ever done is love you, provide for you, try to guide you. And this is how you repay us? No contact, no explanation, no respect for everything we've sacrificed?"

Then, my father again: "Enough is enough. You will call us back today, or we're coming to check on you ourselves. We need to know you're safe, at the very least."

The voicemail ends. I stare at my phone, my professional triumph already fading under the familiar weight of guilt and obligation.

But something's different this time. I just got my first byline. I'm building something real with Nils. I'm finally starting to like who I am.

I'm strong enough for this.

Before I can lose my nerve, I call them back.

"Finally," my father answers. No hello, no concern. Just judgment. It fuels my resolve.

"I'm fine," I say, proud of how steady my voice is. "I've just had a lot going on."

"Too much to return your parents' calls? To show basic courtesy?"

I take a breath. What I don't say: I'm sorry. Because I'm not. Not anymore.

"I needed some space to figure things out."

"Figure what out? We've paved the way for a bright future for you, young lady, and all you needed to do was trust us." His voice hardens. "Speaking of which, do you have any idea how embarrassed we were when David showed up for your date and you weren't there?"

"I told you I was canceling —"

"The morning of! After we'd already arranged everything. We assumed you'd come to your senses! That young man comes from a good family, Alexsis. He would be a perfect husband. But you can't even give him the courtesy of meeting him."

"I don't want a perfect husband chosen by you," I say quietly. "I want to choose my own partner."

Silence. Then he says, "What does that mean?" His tone is hard and cold.

I take a deep breath. "I'm seeing someone."

"Who?" my mother asks, her voice sharp with interest. "What's his name? What ward is he in? What does he do?"

"He makes me happy. That's all you need to know."

"All we need to know?" My father's voice rises. "Young lady, you do not get to —"

"I'm twenty-two years old," I interrupt. "I'm an adult. I get to decide what information I share and when."

The silence that follows is deafening.

"If you're seeing someone seriously enough to refuse dates with appropriate suitors," my mother finally says, "then the least you can do is bring him to Sunday lunch so we can meet him."

I close my eyes. I knew this was coming. "Fine. We'll be there Sunday."

"We'll see you at noon," my father says coldly, and hangs up.

I immediately text Aiden.

Can you meet today? Need to talk.

His response is instant.

Everything okay? Coffee in an hour?

An hour later, I'm sitting across from my brother at a hipster coffee shop in WeHo, far from anywhere our parents would venture.

"You look stressed," he observes, sliding a lavender latte toward me.

"I just got off the phone with Mom and Dad."

He winces. "How bad was it?"

"Pretty bad. They were doing the whole guilt trip thing about me not calling, not coming to lunch, not pretending I give a shit about dating every Mormon boy they throw at me." I take a sip of the latte, letting the familiar comfort wash over me. "I told them I'm seeing someone."

Aiden's eyebrows rise. "Seriously?"

"They insisted I bring him to lunch Sunday."

"Him being ...?"

I meet his eyes. "Nils."

A slow smile spreads across his face. "I knew it. I mean, I strongly suspected after that lunch, but —"

"It was still new then," I clarify.

"Ah. So how long have you been dating?"

"A little over a month?" I estimate. Time feels fluid when it comes to Nils. Like we've been together forever and also like it's still brand new.

"And you're happy?"

The question catches me off guard with its simplicity. "Yeah. Really happy. He's ..." I search for words. "He sees me, you know? The real me. And he doesn't run away."

Aiden reaches across the table and squeezes my hand. "Good. You deserve that."

"Thanks." I squeeze back. "But Sunday's going to be rough. Bringing him as my actual boyfriend? They're going to have questions. Expectations."

"You want me to run interference?"

I shake my head. "I appreciate it, but you have your own secrets to protect. I don't want to put you in the position of defending me and potentially outing yourself."

His face softens. "Lex—"

"No." I hold up a hand. "I mean it. I know how hard it is, keeping parts of yourself hidden from them. I'm not going to make it harder."

He's quiet for a moment. "Josh and I are talking about getting married."

"Aiden!" I reach for his hand again. "That's amazing. I'm so happy for you."

"Thanks. But it means ..." He trails off.

"It means you'll have to tell them eventually."

"Or never see them again." The pain in his voice is evident. Pain I know well. But Aiden is so much stronger than I am. He's always been the quiet but steady and determined one.

"Hey." I wait until he meets my eyes. "Whatever

you decide, whenever you decide it, I've got your back. Just like you've got mine."

He smiles, but it's sad. "How did we end up here? Hiding who we are from the people who supposedly love us most?"

"Because their love comes with conditions," I say simply. "Ones we could never meet."

We sit with that truth for a moment.

"So," Aiden finally says, "you need to tell Nils he's meeting the parents. As your boyfriend this time."

I groan. "I know. He was so good about it last time, pretending we barely knew each other. This is going to be so much worse."

"Maybe not. At least you don't have to pretend."

"No, just hide the fact that I'm a rock journalist who used to do porn and frequents sex clubs." I laugh, but it's hollow. "You know, totally normal dinner conversation."

Aiden's brows jump. "I'm sorry, you used to do what and you frequent where?"

I cover my laugh so I don't spit lavender latte all over him. I didn't mean to confess so nonchalantly. "You heard me," I say after I've swallowed.

Aiden leans back in his chair. "Wow. I mean ... I

got the impression you went a little wild after you left home, but I didn't realize it went *that* far."

I scrunch my nose. "Are you disappointed in me?"

Aiden reaches out and takes my hand. "God, no, Lex, I could never be disappointed in you. We all have to experience life before we figure out who we really are." He pauses. "So you're not still doing …" he lowers his voice to a whisper "… porn, are you?"

I bite into my bottom lip to keep from busting out laughing. "No. That was a phase. But I'm not going to pretend I still don't have kinks." I wink at him.

Now it's his turn to wrinkle his nose. "Ew. Didn't really need to know that about my sister, but okay. You do you. And yeah. So you may have to do *some* pretending at lunch after all."

I sigh. "Yeah. I mean, it's not like *those* things will come up. Really, the problem is, I'm tired of it. I'm tired of being two different people. I just want to be me."

"I know the feeling." He glances at his phone. "And I hate to say I have to cut the conversation here. I really have to head back to work. But Lex? I'm proud of you. For standing up to them. For going after what you want."

"Thanks." I stand and hug him tight. "Love you."

"Love you, too. Good luck with Nils."

I wave as he heads out, staying to finish my coffee before heading back to work myself.

I know I should text Nils now so we can meet up, but I also know he's holding a special event at Baltia tonight. Some sort of charity concert. So, he'll be busy. And I don't want to distract him from something so important.

I sigh as I chuck my now-empty coffee cup into the recycling. I'm still lying to myself. Because I'm already anxious about telling him what went down with my parents. And whether he'll even want to go with me. I should've asked him *before* I agreed he'd go. But I know him. He will because I said he would, and he wouldn't want to make things harder for me with my parents. But I feel like it's a lot to ask, after everything he's already given.

I have to stop myself from thinking I don't deserve that kind of love.

But then I realize, I do. And I'm going to show the people who never gave it to me, who wanted to arrange a future where I'd likely never have it, that I don't just deserve that kind of love, I have it. How they respond will decide whether I allow them in my life going forward. But I finally realize I don't need them anymore. In fact, I may be better off without them, just like Nils once said.

I know it's true, deep down. I probably even knew it then, I just needed to come to the realization on my own. Even though it makes me feel sad and strong in equal measure. It reminds me of that song that wonders if devotion is a gift or a thief … I'm learning it can be either. You just have to be careful who you're devoted to.

22

NILS

The charity concert is in full swing when I spot Emma weaving through the crowd. She's dressed to kill in a black minidress and heels, her blond hair loose around her shoulders. But what catches my attention is the tall guy trailing behind her — also blond, lean in the musician sort of way, with tattoos snaking down both arms.

Something about him seems familiar, but I can't place it in the dim lighting and chaos of the packed club.

I watch them find space on the dance floor, Emma grinding against him with an enthusiasm that makes me raise an eyebrow. Well, good for her. Maybe getting laid regularly will help with her attitude at work.

I'm about to turn my attention back to the sound levels when Marco, one of my bartenders, appears at my elbow.

"Boss, we got a problem. Customer says we overcharged his card by like two hundred bucks."

I sigh. "Show me."

The next twenty minutes are spent sorting out what turns out to be a simple case of the customer misreading his own receipt — he'd bought rounds for his entire group and forgotten. By the time I've smoothed things over with a complimentary drink, Emma and her mystery man have vanished from the dance floor.

The rest of the night passes in the usual controlled chaos of a successful event. The bands are tight, the crowd is generous with their donations, and we raise a decent amount for the local music education charity. By the time we're closing down, I'm exhausted but satisfied.

I head to my office to grab my things, already thinking about crawling into bed with Alexsis. The door is closed, which is odd — I'm sure I left it open. I push it open without thinking.

"Oh, for fuck's sake," I exclaim at the sight that greets me.

Emma is bent over my desk, her dress hiked up

around her waist, while the blond guy pounds into her from behind. They both freeze at my voice.

"Seriously?" I ask, more amused than annoyed.

Emma looks my way, and instead of the mortification I expect, she grins. "Now we're even," she pants.

The blond guy pulls out and turns, and I finally recognize him. Ward from Violent Mood Swings, his face flushed and his impressive cock still hard.

I lean against the doorframe and raise an eyebrow. "How exactly does this make us even? Didn't you know? I *like* to watch."

Emma's face goes bright red as she realizes her revenge plan has backfired. She scrambles to pull her dress down. "I — that's not — dammit!"

Ward, meanwhile, bursts out laughing. "Want to join us, mate? I don't mind sharing."

"Ward!" Emma smacks his arm. "Absolutely not. No way. We're leaving. Right now."

She grabs her purse and storms past me, her face still flaming. Ward follows more leisurely, not bothering to look embarrassed as he tucks himself back into his jeans.

I can't help but laugh as she stalks down the hallway.

"Good to see you, man," Ward says, pausing

beside me. "Though I didn't expect you to see quite so much of me."

"Likewise," I reply drily. "Though I have to admit, Emma's revenge attempt was creative."

Ward grins. "She seemed to think giving you a taste of your own medicine would embarrass you." He shrugs. "Guess she doesn't know you very well."

"Guess not. Tell her to consider us even now." I pause. "I didn't know you two were dating."

"It's pretty new," Ward admits. "We've been seeing each other for a month or two. But I really like her. She's a firecracker."

"That's one word for it," I mutter.

Ward laughs. "She said you two have been butting heads at work."

"Bit of an understatement." I consider my words carefully. "We made peace, but apparently she still felt like we needed a level playing field." Ward smirks. "Look, she's smart and capable. She just needs to relax a little. Stop trying so hard to prove herself. I've told her this over and over, but maybe she'll listen if you tell her."

"I'll see what I can do," Ward says with a wink. "And maybe if I fuck her over her own desk a few more times, that'll help her mellow out."

"One can hope," I reply. "Just ... maybe lock the door next time?"

"Where's the fun in that?" He claps me on the shoulder. "See you around, Nils."

After he leaves, I survey my violated desk and shake my head. At least they didn't knock anything over. I'll have to sanitize the hell out of it tomorrow, though.

I check my phone and find texts from Alexsis from about an hour ago.

Can you come by after work?

I know it'll be late but I really need to see you

I check the time — nearly three a.m. But her last text was only twenty minutes ago. I send her one of my own.

Just closing up. It'll be closer to 4 by the time I get there. That okay?

Her response is immediate.

Yes please. I'll be in bed.

That last line makes me close up a little faster.

The drive to her place is quiet, the streets mostly empty except for other night shift workers and the occasional drunk stumbling home. I use the key she gave me for just these kinds of nights to let myself in, finding her curled up in bed in one of my T-shirts she'd stolen.

"Hey," she says softly, lifting the comforter and patting the empty spot next to her.

I lean down and kiss her on the forehead. "As inviting as that offer is, trust me — you really want me to shower before I get in there," I remind her.

She smiles sleepily and nods. I head into her bathroom for a quick rinse off and I slide on a fresh pair of boxer briefs before heading back.

Her eyes are closed, so I get into bed as carefully as I can, but her eyes instantly pop back open.

I smile and pull her into my arms. "Everything okay?"

She takes a deep breath. "My parents called. Well, left another voicemail. I called them back."

I tense slightly, rubbing my thumb over her back. "And?"

"And I told them I'm seeing someone — I didn't tell them who. They want me to bring him — you — to lunch on Sunday."

I pull back to look at her face. "As your boyfriend this time."

"Yes." She searches my eyes. "Is that ... are you okay with that?"

"Of course I am," I say immediately. "But are you sure you want to do this? Last time was hard enough, and we were just pretending to be acquaintances."

"I know." She fidgets with the waistband of my underwear. "But I'm tired of lying to them. Tired of being two different people."

I study her face, seeing the determination there beneath the nervousness. "There might be a way to avoid a complete fallout," I offer carefully.

Her brows furrow. "What do you mean?"

"I've been thinking a lot about this. I could convert. Become Mormon. Maybe then they'd accept us."

Her eyes go wide. "You'd do that? For me?"

"If it meant you could have both — me and your family — then yes," I reply without hesitation.

She's quiet for a long moment, and when she speaks, her voice is thick with emotion. "They'd see right through it. My dad especially. And even if they didn't, they still wouldn't approve. You're not from the lifestyle, you're twelve years older than me, we've already been seeing each other unchaperoned ..." She shakes her head. "But the fact that you'd even consider it ..." She cups my face in her hands. "You matter to me, Nils. You matter so much. And I've always told myself that someday, when I found something that really mattered, I'd be honest with them."

My heart pounds as she continues.

"I love you," she says tenderly, looking deep into my eyes. "I love you, and I don't want to lie to my parents about that. I want to tell them we're together, that I'm not going to marry a good Mormon boy, even if it means losing them."

I pull her against me, overwhelmed at her declaration. "You love me?"

She nods against my chest. "I realized that maybe you were right. That losing them wouldn't be such a bad thing. It would hurt, but I'd be free. Free to be myself, to live authentically, without keeping secrets or telling lies. Free to love you without hiding in shame."

"Alexsis." I tilt her chin up. "I'm so proud of you. And I love you, too. So much."

She kisses me then, soft and deep, and I taste tears on her lips. When we break apart, I brush them away with my thumbs.

"We'll face them together," I promise. "Whatever happens."

"Together," she agrees, closing her eyes. "You have no idea how much I want that."

"You know what I want right now?" I ask huskily, sliding my hand under her shirt.

She arches against me and mewls. "Tell me," she breathes. "Or better — show me."

So, I do. I slip my hand lower, only to find she's not wearing panties. I groan as my fingers find her pussy slick and ready for me.

I don't waste it.

I roll onto my back, pulling her onto my stomach while I shimmy off my underwear. Then I slide her back onto my cock, impaling her without preamble. She gasps, leaning forward with her hands on my pecs. She rocks her hips over mine, adjusting. And as soon as she does, she sits up, whisks off her top and brings my hands to her breasts.

I knead and work them as she moves over me, chasing her pleasure. I watch her, fascinated, as her beautiful lips purse while my cock moves inside her.

"God, I love you," I breathe.

She pinches her eyes closed, fucking me harder. I pull at her nipples, helping her peak.

"I love you," I repeat, testing a theory. She breathes harder, goes faster.

She gets off on my declaration.

Fuck. I thicken inside her, getting just as turned on as she is.

We repeat the cycle over and over. Until our bodies are working in tandem to climb higher and higher.

This feels different from all the times before. She loves me. She's choosing me, choosing us, even knowing what it might cost her. And it's bringing an intensity to sex that we've never had.

The next time, it's her who whispers, "I love you," as she comes apart on top of me, her walls clamping down on my cock, bringing me right alongside her.

"I love you," I reply, following her over the edge.

She collapses onto my chest, and I stroke her back. We lay there silently. Me, basking in hearing her confess her love. But by the slight tension that's still in her shoulders, I'm pretty sure that brain of hers is still thinking too much.

"What is it?" I ask.

She leans up, resting her chin on my sternum. "Just ... thank you. For being willing to convert. Even if it wouldn't work, the fact that you'd even be willing to try ..."

"I'd do anything for you," I tell her honestly. "But I'm glad you want to do this on your terms. To be yourself."

"It's taken me long enough to figure out who that is," she says wryly.

"You're worth the wait," I assure her.

She slides off of me, not even caring when our combined come slides down our thighs. "Even if Sunday is a complete disaster? Even if they disown me?"

"Even then." I brush her hair back from her face. "We'll build our own family. You, me, Aiden, when he's ready. The friends who accept us as we are."

Fresh tears well in her eyes. "How did I get so lucky?"

"I'm the lucky one," I correct her, disentangling to grab a washcloth.

I wet and warm it, cleaning her, then myself, before sliding back into bed. She snuggles close to me, and I can feel her heart beating against my side. She idly plays with my cock, and I smile, closing my hand over hers.

"Let's get some sleep. We have a few days to prepare for Sunday."

She settles back against me, humming sleepily, and I feel her body gradually relax into sleep. But I lie awake for a while longer, thinking about what's coming. Her parents won't take this well — I knew that even before she dismissed the conversion idea.

But she's ready to face them, to stand up for herself and what she wants.

I press a kiss to her hair. Whatever happens Sunday, we'll handle it together.

And maybe, just maybe, she'll finally be free.

23

ALEXSIS

My hands are shaking as Nils and I walk up to my parents' front door. He squeezes my fingers gently, and I look up at him. He's dressed conservatively in dark brown slacks and a cream-colored button-down, but there's no hiding what he is — gorgeous, confident, and decidedly not Mormon. Even my own outfit — snug jeans and a long-sleeved red top — is too fitted to be "appropriate" by my parents' definition.

"You ready for this?" he asks softly.

"No," I admit. "But I'm doing it anyway." He grins and squeezes my hand.

And the door opens before we can knock. My mother stands there, her face lighting up when she sees us.

"Nils! What a lovely surprise." She turns to me. "Alexsis, dear, come in. When will your gentleman friend be arriving?"

I take a deep breath. Here we go.

"Mom, Nils is the man I've been seeing."

The smile freezes on her face. Behind her, I see my father rise from his recliner, his expression darkening. I can see Aiden and Asher setting the dining table beyond where my dad sits, and both look like they'd rather be anywhere else.

"I'm sorry, what?" Mom's voice has gone up an octave.

"Nils is my boyfriend," I say clearly, stepping inside with him.

The silence that follows is deafening. My father's face has gone from red to purple, while my mother looks like I've slapped her.

"This is a joke," Dad finally says, staring me down, daring me to contradict him.

"It's not a joke," Nils says calmly. "I care very much for your daughter."

Dad's eyes snap to him, and if looks could kill, Nils would be ash. "You don't speak unless spoken to in my house."

"Dad!" I protest, but Aiden catches my eye and

subtly shakes his head. Pick your battles, his expression says.

"Now, Ammon, let's … well, let's at least just go ahead and have lunch. We'll all be thinking more clearly on a full stomach," my mother says tensely.

So, we move to the dining room in the world's most awkward processional. As we sit, Aiden leans close.

"I told Asher the basics so he wouldn't be blindsided," he whispers. "Hope that's okay."

"Of course," I whisper back, reaching out and squeezing his hand to show him that I'm thankful for the support. I also give Asher a grateful smile.

Mom serves lunch with mechanical precision. Unfortunately, her famous pork loin roast tastes like cardboard in my mouth. I don't know if it's nerves or an actual failure on her part to live up to her own standards, given that she's apparently been beyond distressed by my behavior for weeks.

For a few minutes, we eat in silence that's broken only by the clink of silverware.

"So," Mom finally ventures, her voice artificially bright, "how long have you two been … dating?"

"About six weeks," I answer.

"And have you had a proper chaperone for your outings?" she follows up.

I almost laugh. "No, Mom. We're adults. We don't need a chaperone."

Dad's fork clatters to his plate. "I'm disappointed in you, Nils. Deeply disappointed. We welcomed you into our home. Treated you like a son. And this is how you repay us? By taking advantage of an impressionable young woman?"

"With all due respect, sir," Nils says evenly, "Alexsis is twenty-two years old. A grown woman capable of making her own choices."

"How dare you —"

"And while I did have reservations at first because of our age difference," Nils continues as if Dad hadn't spoken, "Alexsis is one of the most mature, intelligent, wonderful women I've ever met. And I love her."

Dad looks like he's about to have a stroke. Mom quickly places a hand on his arm.

"Alexsis, sweetheart," she says in that tone that means she's about to be condescending, "this can't possibly be a real relationship. He's far too old for you. He's taking advantage of your naivety. And he's not even Mormon, so where could this possibly go?"

This is it. The moment of truth.

"I don't consider myself Mormon either," I say quietly but firmly.

Aiden, Asher, and my mother all suck in sharp breaths.

"What?" my mother demands.

"I haven't lived within the faith since I left home. I only come to church to make you happy, but it's not what I believe. It's not the life I want," I explain.

"Then what life do you want?" Dad's voice is dangerously low.

"One where I make my own choices. Where I can be with who I want to be with. Where I can pursue the career I want."

"You have a career," Mom says. "At that magazine."

"That music magazine," Dad adds with disgust.

"It's a rock music magazine," I clarify. "I'm a journalist at *Rock Scene*."

Both of their faces go white, then red.

"Rock music?" Mom gasps. "You told us it was reputable! Rock is … is … it's the *devil's* music!"

I have to resist rolling my eyes. "It is reputable. It's small, but still one of the best in the industry."

"You lied to us," Dad growls.

"Of course I lied to you!" The words explode out of me. "Because I couldn't bear to hurt your feelings. Because I knew it might mean losing you. But this is who I am, and I don't want to lie anymore." I stand, my whole body shaking. "You either love me enough to accept me for who I am, or you never really loved me at all."

"How dare you question our love!" Dad roars, rising to his feet. "We've given you everything! A pleasant home, strong values, a path to right-eousness! And you throw it all away for what? For a satanic career and fornication with a man old enough to —"

"Stop." Everyone turns to stare at Aiden, who's also standing now. "Just stop, Dad," he says quietly. "You want to talk about lies? About disappointment? Fine. I'm gay."

The word hangs in the air with the stink of Dad's worst fear coming true.

"I've known since I was eight years old," Aiden continues, his voice gaining strength. "I haven't lived within the faith since I was a teenager, either. And I'm engaged to a man named Josh who I love more than anything in this world."

Mom makes a sound like a wounded animal. Dad's face has gone beyond purple to something approaching black.

"No son of mine —" Dad starts.

"Then I guess I'm not your son," Aiden cuts in simply.

"If you're disowning Aiden, then you should disown me, too," Asher suddenly announces. Everyone turns to him. "Katie and I have been living together for years. In sin, as you'd call it. And she's pregnant."

I gasp, then immediately cross to hug him. "Asher! Congratulations!"

He hugs me back, tears in his eyes. I turn and hug Aiden as well, all three of us standing together while our parents look on in horror.

"This is ... this can all be fixed," Mom says desperately. "We'll get counseling at church. Prayer. The bishop can —"

"Katie's Jewish," Asher interrupts. "She has no intention of converting. And neither do I, because I don't believe anymore either. I haven't for a long time."

"Then you're also no son of mine," Dad spits.

I laugh. I can't help it. The absurdity of it all just hits me.

"Seriously? That's all it takes? Asher living with his pregnant Jewish fiancée gets him disowned, but me dating Nils isn't enough?" I shake my head. "Well, let me make it easier for you. I also did porn to pay for college."

Mom stands abruptly. "Stop it. You're just saying that to scandalize us."

"Am I? How did you think I afforded a private university on a part-time internship? It's not like you could have helped, not with all your money going to the church."

"You ... you're a nymphomaniac! An abomination!" Dad sputters.

"The term is hypersexual," I correct him. "But that's not accurate either, in my case, anyway. My sexuality doesn't control my life. I'm perfectly productive. I just happen to enjoy kinky sex with strangers."

"Alexsis!" Mom shrieks.

"What? You wanted honesty, right? Fine. Here's some more honesty for you. I'm done hiding. I'm done pretending to be the perfect Mormon daughter you want me to be. And clearly, you're never going to accept that your children don't fit the obedient little mold your religion demands."

I move back to Nils, who rises and takes my hand.

"So here's the deal," I continue. "If you ever figure out what's really important in this world — your actual children, not the imaginary ones you wish you had — I'll be willing to accept your apology. For making me feel unloved and imperfect my whole life. For making all of us hide who we really are. But until then? You can fuck right off."

The profanity in their sacred dining room is the final straw. Mom sinks into her chair while Dad stands there, mouth opening and closing like a fish.

"We're leaving," I announce. Nils squeezes my hand in solidarity.

"Right behind you," Aiden says.

Asher hesitates for a second, looking at our parents. Then he shakes his head and follows us out without a word.

The moment we're outside, the adrenaline crashes, and I start laughing and crying at the same time. My brothers pull me into a group hug, and I feel Nils's hand on my back.

"Holy shit," Asher breathes. "We actually did it."

"Thank you," I manage through my tears. "Thank you both for standing with me."

"Are you kidding?" Aiden asks. "Thank *you*. I've wanted to do that for years."

"That was ..." Asher shakes his head. "Long overdue. All of it."

We stand there in our parents' driveway, outcasts who've finally found the courage to be ourselves.

"I have to go home and tell Josh about this, but

we should meet up soon," Aiden says. "All of us. With Josh and Katie, too."

"Absolutely," I agree. "And if Mom and Dad come around ..."

"We'll deal with that if it happens," Asher says. "Though I doubt it will." We all nod in agreement, then exchange one more round of hugs, heading to our separate cars.

As Nils steps aside to say his goodbyes to Aiden, I look back at the house where I grew up. Where I learned to hide. Where I learned to lie.

Nils comes back to me, placing a hand on my back. "Are you okay?" he asks softly.

I turn to him, this man who loves me enough to face my parents, to offer to convert for me, to stand by me as I burned that bridge to ashes.

"Yeah," I say, and realize I mean it. "I am. I'm finally free."

He lifts our joined hands and kisses my knuckles. "Yes, you are."

As we drive away, I don't look back. There's nothing there for me anymore. My real family — the one that loves me as I am — is right here beside me.

And for the first time in my life, that's enough.

24

———————

NILS

As Alexsis heads to the car, Aiden catches my arm.

"Hey, can I talk to you for a second?" he asks, looking nervous.

I glance at Alexsis, who nods. "Of course," I respond, following him a few paces away from his sister.

He shifts uncomfortably, then meets my eyes with determination. "I wanted to say … you should tell her everything. About us. I don't want to be another secret waiting to detonate."

My eyebrows rise. "Aiden —"

"I mean it," he interrupts. "You two are perfect for each other. And I don't want there to be anything hidden between you because of me. She deserves to know. She deserves a relationship where *no one* has to hide."

I study his face, seeing the sincerity there. "You're sure? It's not like we've discussed other past lovers."

"I'm sure. Because this is different, and I think you know it. Just ... maybe leave out the graphic details?" He manages a wry smile. "I don't need my sister knowing everything about my sex life from when I was seventeen."

I huff a laugh. "Fair enough. And you're right. I wouldn't want her to somehow learn about it another way. Thank you. For this. And for standing up in there. That took real courage."

"I think we all found our courage today." He glances back at the house. "Better late than never, right?"

We shake hands, then embrace briefly.

"Take care of her," he says as we part.

"Always," I promise.

In the car, Alexsis is practically vibrating with a mixture of emotions — relief, sadness, anger, and something that looks like joy.

"I can't believe we did that," she says as I pull away from the curb. "I can't believe they all stood with me. God, poor Aiden. And Asher! And oh my god, they're having a baby!" She puts her hands to her cheeks and shakes her head, clearly over-whelmed.

"Your brothers love you," I point out. "Of course they stood with you."

"I know, but still." She lets out a long, slow breath. "I feel like I should feel worse about this. About losing my parents. But mostly I just feel... free."

"You are free," I confirm. "Free to be yourself. All of yourself."

She's quiet for a moment. "Speaking of which, there's something I need to tell you."

My hands tighten on the wheel, remembering Aiden's words. "Actually, there's something I need to tell you first."

"Oh?" She turns in her seat to face me.

"About Aiden and me." I take a breath. "When I was living with your family, we ... we had a brief thing. Nothing serious, just two confused teenagers figuring things out. But I thought you should know."

There's a beat of silence, then Alexsis bursts out laughing.

"Are you serious right now?" she manages between giggles.

I glance at her, confused by her reaction. "Yes?"

"That's fucking awesome!" She's practically cackling now. "You've been part of the sexual awakening of two Monaghans. We should get you a plaque or a medal or something."

"I'm not sure that's the reaction I expected," I admit, a smile tugging at my lips.

"What, did you think I'd be upset? Jealous?" She shakes her head. "Nils, that's hilarious and kind of perfect. No wonder Aiden was so supportive from the start."

Relief washes through me. "He told me to tell you. He didn't want any secrets between us. And neither do I."

"You're both good men." She reaches over and takes my hand. "No secrets. Which brings me to what I wanted to say."

I squeeze her fingers. "I'm listening."

"I've been thinking a lot about us. About what we have." She pauses, seeming to gather her thoughts. "My whole adult life, I've been two people. Alexsis Monaghan, the good girl pretending for her parents. And Tessa Temptation, the sexual being who takes what she wants."

"And now?"

"Now I've found someone who accepts both. Who sees all of me and doesn't disown me." She turns our joined hands over, studying them. "I'd like to try something I've never been open to before."

My pulse quickens. "What's that?"

"Monogamy." The word hangs in the air between us. "True commitment. Setting aside sex with anyone else. Just us."

I pull over to the side of the road, needing to focus on this conversation fully. "Alexsis ..."

"I know what I said when this started," she rushes on. "About not being capable of it. But that was before I knew what it felt like to be truly seen. Truly loved."

I turn to face her fully. "I need you to understand something. I never needed you to change for me. I just wanted you to admit your feelings. To acknowledge that what we have is special enough to commit to."

"I know," she says softly. "And it is. God, it really is."

"And commitment doesn't mean we can't involve others sometimes," I continue carefully. "It just means it looks different. It's us together, choosing together. Not you seeking something I'm not giving you."

Her eyes brighten. "You mean like at the club? When we played together?"

"Exactly like that. If and when we both want it."

She unbuckles her seatbelt and slides across to straddle my lap, the steering wheel digging into her back. "I love you," she says, cupping my face. "I love you so much it scares me sometimes."

"I love you, too," I reply, pulling her down for a kiss. "And I promise, we'll figure this out together. What works for us. What we both need."

She kisses me deeply, and I lose myself in the taste of her, the feel of her. When we finally break apart, we're both breathing hard.

"Take me home," she whispers. "I want to celebrate our freedom. Our future. Us."

I help her back to her seat, my body already responding to the promise in her voice. The drive to my apartment is charged with anticipation.

The moment we're inside, she's on me, pushing me against the door and attacking the buttons of my shirt.

"Where are the rest of your sex toys?" she says against my throat. "I know the vibrators we've used can't be everything you've got."

I groan. "Bedroom closet. Top shelf."

She pulls back with a wicked grin. "Race you there."

She bolts toward the bedroom. I chuckle and

head to the kitchen, grabbing a couple of glasses of water before leisurely joining her. I find her riffling through the bin, eyes wide, biting that luscious bottom lip of hers. She looks up as I set the glasses down on the nightstand.

"You've been holding out on me. This is quite the collection," she comments.

I raise a brow. "I didn't want to spring it on you all at once. I take it that means you approve?" I tease.

She grins. "Naturally." She holds up a set of silk restraint ties, complete with matching blindfold. "And I know exactly what I want you to do to me."

"You want me to blindfold you and tie you up?" I ask, my cock hardening even saying the words.

She nods slowly, setting the rest of the bin on the floor and tossing the silk bundle my way. And then she strips. Slowly. Tantalizingly. And crawls across the bed toward me, naked, her nipples hard, her pupils dilated. Needless to say, it makes me rock hard for her.

I lift the silk blindfold and run it down her chest, over her nipple.

"Are you sure about this?" I ask. "This will give me total control over you. I can touch you any way I want. Do whatever I want. I could keep you from coming for hours while I torture you."

"I trust you," she says, undoing the last few buttons of my shirt.

I wrap my hand around hers, and take both of her hands, guiding her to lay down on the bed.

"Close your eyes."

She complies and I kiss each eyelid before blindfolding her. And then I tie each wrist and ankle to the four corners of the bed frame. I step back, and suck in a sharp breath at the sight of her, spread out on my bed, her sex already glistening with her arousal. Her lips are parted, she's panting, and her hard nipples are peaked on her perfect breasts.

I grab a long feather from the bin and trace it slowly up her body, from toe … to knee … over her sex and all the way up to her chin. She arches beautifully as it tickles her face.

"You are a work of art," I tell her, placing a light kiss on her lips.

She squirms, clearly ready for more, and I chuckle, reaching down to pinch a nipple.

"Patience, my love," I say softly in her ear. "Don't worry. I'll give you what you need."

I return the feather to my stash in favor of a bullet vibrator. I turn it on, and she whimpers at the gentle humming noise. I likewise run it up her body, skipping her pussy this time, and running it around her nipples each in turn before settling it on her bottom lip. She licks it, but I only allow it for a moment before quickly dropping it to her clit, working it in gentle but firm circles.

"Yes," she hisses. And I remove it. She whimpers. And I touch it back to her sex.

I let it stimulate her until she's making the noises I know mean she's going to come … and I pull it away. She makes a deeper noise of frustration, and I chuckle.

I answer by undressing, making sure to audibly lower my zipper. That gets a sharp intake of breath from her. Once I'm naked, I loosen the ties on her ankles enough to put her knees up, then tighten them again.

I run a fingertip over the path the feather and vibrator had taken. One single digit. Goosebumps break out over her skin along the path that I touch.

"So sensitive," I murmur. When I get to her face, I climb on the bed, leaning in so my hard cock grazes her lips. "Suck it, Alexsis. Show me what a good girl you are, and I'll reward you."

Without hesitation, she takes me into her mouth, her tongue swirling around the head before she takes me to the back of her throat. I groan involuntarily at the wet warmth of her mouth, my balls tightening at the sudden shift.

"Brace yourself, älskling." I give her a mere moment before I move, fucking her mouth, holding nothing back.

She drools and gags but keeps bobbing on my cock in time with my thrusts. I get within a hair's edge of coming in her beautiful mouth before I pull back. I lean in, letting out my desire with my mouth on hers, tongue fucking her where my cock had just been doing the same. She returns in kind with the same desperation I feel to be inside her.

But not yet.

Instead, I drop between her legs, using only my tongue to lightly trace her nether lips. She gasps and stills, allowing me to slowly slip between her folds. To trace her entrance. To flick her clit. And again, with more pressure. Her hips buck. I add a finger, sliding it slowly into her dripping pussy before flexing it lightly as I flick her clit with my tongue. I keep going, slowly adding pressure and speed on both ends. Until I unleash, fucking her hard and fast from both directions and she comes instantly, gushing onto my waiting tongue.

"Fuck," she groans as I wring the last of her

orgasm out of her with my finger. "I need more, Nils. I need your cock inside me."

"I need that, too," I promise as I untie her restraints. And then I give myself to her. I seat myself at her entrance and push in, smoothly and completely as her arms and legs wrap around me. I let go, slamming my cock into her over and over, tasting her with my tongue, feeling her with my hands over her skin.

We move together with an intensity we never have before. With a deep trust and newfound joy. It's freedom and connection and love all wrapped up in sweat-slicked skin and breathless moans.

I feel myself getting close, but I don't want it to end. So, holding her tightly to me, I roll and put her on top. She pushes up her blindfold and looks down at me with such love in her eyes that it makes my chest and cock ache at once. She watches me as she swirls her hips over me. At least, until the pleasure is too much. Then she leans forward, chasing her high. I pump into her from beneath, feeling her walls flutter.

"Give it to me, Alexsis," I beg. "Give me all of you. All of that pussy. I need it." She whimpers and twists her hips faster while I pound into her harder. "That's it, älskling. That's my good girl. Get yourself off on my cock."

She gasps — at my words, at the insane pleasure, or both — and her brows pinch together, her lips parting. So I go faster, knowing how close she is.

"Fuck, I'm going to come inside you," I grunt.

And that tips her over the edge. She comes with me, tightening around my emptying cock, wringing every last drop from me as she shatters, crying out.

Finally, exhausted and sated, we collapse together on the thoroughly destroyed bed.

"Holy fuck," Alexsis pants. "Why were we going to sex clubs when we could do this?"

I chuckle, letting her slide down and pulling her against my side. "You say that like we can't have both." I pause. "Don't you miss it? The club, I mean?"

She's quiet for a moment. "Sometimes," she admits. "But I don't want to complicate things. I'm happy with how we are right now." She pinches my nipple playfully. "Very happy."

"Me, too," I say, trailing my fingers down her spine. "But if I'm honest, *I* miss it sometimes."

She props herself up on an elbow. "You do?"

"The energy. The freedom. The way you look when you're in that space. I still dream about the way we fucked at Chained."

Alexsis arches against me. "That was … something," she admits breathlessly.

I smirk down at her. "I did have an idea."

"Oh?" Her eyes light with interest

I roll toward her, kissing her lightly. "But I need to do some research before I share it."

She narrows her eyes. "Are you keeping secrets?"

I grin. "I promise it's one you'll like. And is it a secret if you know it's a secret?"

Her brows pull together. "That's … I don't know," she admits. We both laugh. "Anyway, I trust you. Just … don't wait too long to tell me or I might have to seduce it out of you."

I nip at her lips. "Still playing dirty, I see."

"Only the good kind of dirty now," she replies with a genuine smile. "No more secrets that make me live two lives. No more lies."

"No more hiding," I agree. "No more pretending. Just us, being exactly who we are."

She kisses me softly. "I love you," she says against my lips. "And I love that we can talk about this. Figure things out together."

As she settles back against me, I think about how far we've come. From that first meeting at Baltia to here, in my bed, planning a future neither of us could have imagined. It hasn't been easy, but the best things rarely are.

"What are you thinking about?" she asks sleepily.

"You," I answer honestly. "Us. How lucky I am."

"We both are," she corrects. "We found each other. Despite everything trying to keep us apart, even if it was me sometimes. We found our way to each other."

I press a kiss to her hair. "It wasn't just you. But yes, what matters is where we are now. And now that I have you, I'm never letting go."

She looks up sleepily. "I think I'd be okay with that," she replies with a self-satisfied smile.

I laugh and kiss her forehead. "Sleep, love."

She mumbles an incoherent response as she drifts off to sleep.

I lie awake a bit longer, planning. My secret project … our next adventure. Our future. A life where we can be exactly who we are, together.

No more secrets. No more lies. Just love, acceptance, and the freedom to be ourselves.

It's more than I ever dared hope for. And it's just the beginning.

SIX MONTHS LATER

Six months. That's all it took to go from Nils's "I have an idea" to standing in the entrance of Temptation, our very own sex club.

The space is perfect — intimate but not cramped, luxurious but not intimidating. Deep purple walls, soft lighting, and rooms designed for every possible desire. The main play room has plush seating areas mixed with more adventurous equipment. There's a couples-only room, a voyeur room with one-way glass, and more, including my personal favorite — the girls-only room where I'll be spending most of tonight as Mistress Temptation.

"You ready for this?" Nils asks, adjusting his

black button-down. He looks good enough to eat, and I make a mental note to do exactly that later.

"More than ready," I assure him, smoothing down my latex dress. It's deep red, hugging every curve, with strategic cutouts that leave little to the imagination. I deserved a killer outfit for my debut as a dominatrix.

"I still can't believe Frankie and Julian are some of our test subjects," I say, watching them enter through the VIP entrance. I tried to get Max to agree to it, too, but it was a little too risqué for her tastes. Her loss.

And Frankie looks like she was born for this. She's stunning in a black corset and leather pants, while Julian ... well, Julian looks like he'd burn the place down if anyone other than his wife so much as breathed in his direction.

"They wanted to christen the toy room," Nils says with a shrug. "Who was I to deny our business partner?"

I laugh. "Just make sure they don't break anything expensive. Their Sunday fuck has gone next level since Frankie was cleared for sex after Bianca was born."

Nils grins at the reminder of our arrangement to

use their erotic soundtrack to fuel our own simultaneous rendezvous. Our little secret.

He shrugs. "That's what insurance is for." He pulls me close for a quick kiss. "Now go. Your subjects await, Mistress."

The next few hours blur together in the best possible way. The girls-only room fills quickly with women eager to explore without male interference or pressure. As Mistress Temptation, I guide, encourage, and occasionally participate. It's empowering in a way I never expected — helping other women embrace their desires, their bodies, their pleasure.

By the time I surface to check on the rest of the club, I'm amazed to find we're at capacity.

"We had to close the doors after an hour," Nils tells me, looking slightly shell-shocked. "Most people are staying all night. I've had to turn away dozens more."

"On our first night?"

"Apparently there was more demand for this than we realized." He glances around at the full rooms, the satisfied faces, the couples reconnecting over shared experiences. "We did good, älskling."

Before I can respond, I realize I'm due back in the girls room, so I give him a quick kiss and make a mental note for later.

After closing time, when the last couple has reluctantly left and the cleaning crew has worked their magic, Nils leads me to his office.

"I believe we have some celebrating to do," he says, unlocking the door.

I step inside and laugh. "You weren't kidding about saving the best toys for yourself."

The office is professional enough — desk, chairs, the usual — but one wall is dedicated to the most impressive collection of high-end toys I've ever seen. And that's saying something.

"These were some of the premium samples the toy company sent over. Only the best for us," he says with a grin, already unbuttoning his shirt.

What follows is a thorough testing of several items from his wall of wonders. By the time we collapse on the wide leather couch he had the fore-sight to include, we're both thoroughly satisfied and slightly dazed.

"That was a perfect opening night," Nils murmurs, tracing lazy patterns on my bare hip.

"Mmm," I agree, remembering what I keep forgetting to mention. "It probably helped that my feature on the club got millions of views."

He props himself up on an elbow. "What?"

"The article I wrote for my magazine? About

Temptation opening?" I grin at his stunned expression. "You didn't know?"

"Why didn't you tell me?"

"I keep getting distracted. We have been a little busy," I point out. "Between the final inspections, staff training, and making sure we had enough supplies ..."

"Millions of views?" He shakes his head in amazement. "No wonder we were slammed. Thank you."

"Thank my readers. Turns out there's a real hunger for shame-free discussions of female sexuality."

My online magazine, launched three months ago with backing from some very progressive investors, has exceeded every expectation. We cover everything from sex toy reviews to ethical porn recommendations, some of which are even available on the site, to honest discussions about desire and pleasure.

"I keep meaning to check out the videos section," Nils admits. "I'm curious what porn catered to women actually looks like."

I laugh. "I know what most people think, and no, it's not all videos of men vacuuming and doing dishes. Though, now that I think about it, that would be hot, too."

Nils chuckles. "Duly noted. So what is it?"

"Focus on female pleasure. Real pleasure, not performance. Multiple camera angles that actually show what's happening to her, not just close-ups of penetration. Actual foreplay. Men who know where the clitoris is." I trace a finger down his chest. "All orientations, too — straight, lesbian, threesomes, orgies. Whatever women want to watch."

His eyes darken. "Speaking of which, I've got some female-focused porn I'd like to film right now."

I raise an eyebrow. "Are you suggesting we make a sex tape?"

"I was joking. I just wanted to go down on you again." He pauses, considering. "But I wouldn't be totally opposed to that ..."

The idea sends a thrill through me. We've done so much together, pushed so many boundaries, but never this.

"Set up your phone," I tell him.

His eyes widen. "Really?"

"Really. But if it ends up online anywhere, I'll kill you."

"It's just for us," he promises, already reaching for his phone. "Our own private collection."

He props it on the desk, checking the angle, and I can't help but laugh at how serious he looks.

"Come here," I beckon. "Let's give us something good to watch later."

He joins me on the couch, and as his lips meet mine, I think about how far we've come. From secrets and lies to complete honesty. From hiding who we are to building a business, and a life, around it. From pushing each other away to being unable to imagine life apart.

"I love you," I whisper against his lips.

"I love you, too," he replies. "Ready?"

I glance at the phone, recording our next adventure, and smile. With Nils, I'm ready for anything. And thankfully, I already know my best angles.

"Always."

Thank you so much for reading! Please take a minute to leave a review on any retailer, goodreads, and/or BookBub. Even if it's just a couple of sentences, your opinion is important to potential readers and to me. Thank you!

Curious about Frankie and Julian? She's a human lie detector and he's the muscle sent to scope her out. Find out how they got together in the steamy psychic romantic suspense novel *Everybody Lies*.

Sign up for Melanie A. Smith's newsletter to get a FREE book plus all the latest news and more
https://melanieasmithauthor.com/newsletter.html

ACKNOWLEDGMENTS

To my husband and son, for letting me disappear so often into fiction, and tolerating my stream-of-consciousness babble about characters and plots and all things writerly. I'm a verbal processor, and I am so grateful they put up with me.

To Erin. Where do I even begin? Friend, encourager, supporter, beta reader, fellow author, and amazing human being, I'm so damn grateful to have you in my life.

To Anne. Please don't arrest me for the level of smut in this book. XD Seriously, though, I couldn't do any of this without your support, advice, and shoulder to lean on. I appreciate you so much!

In writing this, I realize my acknowledgments have gotten shorter over the years as my community does. A mix of my personality, life, and the evolution of the author/book community have tightened my circle to those few who I know I can trust. The flip side is, it's made the support of readers like you even more important to me. And that, I think, is as it should be, because it's you, dear reader, that matters most. So I hope you enjoyed this super steamy departure from my more recent work. I simply went where the characters took me, and I appreciate you coming along on the journey.

ABOUT THE AUTHOR

Melanie A. Smith is an award-winning, international best-selling author of steamy romance with smart, self-sufficient heroines and strong, swoony book boyfriends with hearts of gold. A former engineer turned stay-at-home mom and author, when Melanie is not lost in the world of books you'll find her spending time with her husband and son, crafting, or cross-stitching.

Connect with Melanie on:

MelanieASmithAuthor.com

facebook.com/MelanieASmithAuthor

instagram.com/melanieasmithauthor

BOOKS BY MELANIE A. SMITH

The Safeguarded Heart Series

The Safeguarded Heart

All of Me

Never Forget

Her Dirty Secret

Recipes from the Heart: A Companion to the Safeguarded
Heart Series

The Safeguarded Heart Complete Series: All Five Books
and Exclusive Bonus Material

Life Lessons

Never Date a Doctor

Bad Boys Don't Make Good Boyfriends

You Can't Buy Love

The Heart of Rutherford: The Complete Life Lessons
Series

Alpine Ridge

Tough Love

Recklessly in Love

Unscripted Love

Elusive Love

TRUE Love: The Alpine Ridge Complete Series

L.A. Rock Scene

Everybody Lies

Finding His Redemption

Secrets, Lies, and Temptation

Stand-alones

Last Kiss Under the Mistletoe

Vegas Baby

Short Stories

Cruising for Love

Hot for Santa